I0691400

WANDA THE WHIP LADY

A BDSM NOVEL

First Edition

Published by The Nazca Plains Corporation
Las Vegas, Nevada
2010

ISBN: 978-1-935509-98-1
E-book: 978-1-61098-005-0

Published by

The Nazca Plains Corporation ®
4640 Paradise Rd, Suite 141
Las Vegas NV 89109-8000

PUBLISHER'S NOTE
Wanda the Whip Lady is a work of fiction created wholly by *Tim Desmondes'* imagination. All characters are fictional and any resemblance to any persons living or deceased is purely by accident. No portion of this book reflects any real person or events.

Cover Model, CherriesJubalie
Cover Photo, Leon MonkeyFetish
Cover Design, Ian Ray
Art Director, Blake Stephens

DEDICATION

This book is dedicated to all masochists.

Your story has been neglected and downplayed for centuries while sadists have had their fictional say since the Marquis de Sade wrote his brilliant novels in the eighteenth century.

So, the following novel is meant to celebrate you, the masochists of the world.

Welcome back into the limelight.

WANDA THE WHIP LADY

A BDSM NOVEL

First Edition

Tim Desmondes

CONTENTS

CONTENTS CONTINUED...

INTRODUCTION

Most novels dealing with BDSM are geared more to the sadistic side of the practice than the masochistic.

The Marquis de Sade's works are the classics in the sadistic genre and his novel *Justine* is one of the world's great classics.

Masochism, the necessary flip-side of the subject, tends to be underplayed in literature.

Leopold von Sacher-Masoch, the nineteenth century Austrian writer, published *Venus in Furs* in 1870. The work instantly became the prime novel celebrating masochism. So, just as the Marquis de Sade's name gave birth to the word *sadism*, so did von Sacher-Masoch's name enter the European languages with the word *masochism*.

Venus in Furs is not an easy read. Nor is it widely read today.

I have translated the book into a twenty-first century setting and have moved the essential story to the American continents. I am hopeful this will make the story more accessible to today's readers.

So get ready to enjoy the pleasures of masochism as you read on.

Because, for the cognoscenti, it is well known that nothing beats a good whipping spiced with jolly humiliation to give a chap a roaring good time.

CHAPTER ONE

BAREFOOT IN ZIHUATANEJO

Where will I begin my story?

Of course, the story really began when one of my father's sperm cells wiggled its little way into my mother's ripe ovum. Because at that moment I became who and what I am. I know that I was already, at that moment, a masochist. And, of course, I remain one to this day.

But rather than launching this story with speculations about my parent's love life, I prefer to begin it some twenty four years later. For I was fully mature when I met Wanda. And, in a sense, that was when *it* all began.

I was on vacation in Zihuatanejo, a tropical town on the west coast of Mexico, when I fell in love.

Although Zihuatanejo is physically located in a region known as the Mexican Riviera, the town is not really a part of it.

Adjacent to Zihuatanejo is the tourist resort town of Ixtapa. It is an area of luxury hotels where the lingua franca is not Spanish but English.

Although I was easily able to walk barefoot from Zihuatanejo to Ixtapa, and frequently did so, the two communities are miles...leagues apart socially, economically and culturally.

I regularly flew down to Zihuatanejo from my home in San Diego when my employer, the San Diego Library System, saw fit to allow me a week or so respite from my arduous duties as an assistant branch librarian.

The flight from San Diego to Zihuatanejo is pleasant enough, with only one stop in Arizona.

I arrived at my destination with a suitcase full of tropical clothing, a supply of linen rope with which to be bound, and carrying my rattan cane in hand. The better to be beaten with.

I always stayed at the Hotel Pancho Villa, which has very low rates. I might even say dirt cheap.

Because the place is a dump.

The hotel is only a block from La Madera Beach.

No one working at the hotel speaks a word of English. Because no Gringo (other than a wretch like me) would ever stay at the dismal place.

My grasp of the Spanish language is adequate. I need to resort to my Spanish-English dictionary with fair regularity to make myself understood. But I generally am able to satisfy my peculiar needs in Zihuatanejo one way or another.

Why did I come to Zihuatanejo for my vacations? Well, chiefly to read porn, to get whipped, abused and fucked by whores, and to jack off under the palm trees by the sea at night.

In short, because I was into "self-abuse" in any sense you wish to take the term.

What I appreciated about the Pancho Villa Hotel was the ease with which I could get whores into my room. Chuy, the proprietor and desk clerk, could always get his "sister," his "sweetheart," or his "neighbor's girl" for me for twenty dollars American. He assured me that each one was barely sixteen years old. And, of course, was a certified virgin.

In person, the "girls" looked more like I imagined Chuy's mother, aunt or grandmother might appear. Fat, ugly and forty plus years of age.

But I have always hated myself. I am replete with self-disgust. So I never felt I deserved better than that.

And, let's face it. What can one expect for twenty bucks a pop?

I want to tell you about an encounter I had on a fateful vacation I took during my twenty-fifth year.

Chuy sent a whore named Fulana to my room.

She was just what I needed. Fat, ugly, fortyish, with fetid breath and a bad attitude.

I had doused myself well with cheap tequila before she arrived. With the combination of the booze and the whore's unattractiveness I could hardly get it up to begin with. But, as it always did, my potency increased with hearty female abuse.

Fulana well knew what I expected from her. Chuy always prepped the whores about the weird desires of the Gringo loco.

Fulana stepped into my room and unattractively disrobed. Her body was less than appealing.

Without so much as a verbal greeting, she went directly to the rickety dresser in the room and picked up the lengths of rope I had waiting for her.

Once she had the ropes in hand she deigned to cast a disdainful glance at the bed where she knew I would be lying naked atop the sheets stroking my prick into as stiff a hardon as I could raise under the circumstances.

I turned over onto my stomach, placing my wrists together behind my back. My pecker was hard enough to make me experience a bit of discomfort from the pressure on it. The aggravation to my staff turned out to be more stimulating, sexually, than the nude woman approaching me.

Like all the whores Chuy had ever sent me, this broad could tie a mean knot. Mexican women of her social caste did lots of tying, tethering and wrapping with rope in their peon lives.

Once she had immobilized my hands behind my back, she brutally yanked me up and onto my feet by the side of the bed.

Still without muttering a word, she jerked her end of the rope down towards the floor, forcing me onto my knees beside the bed, as though I was preparing to say my prayers.

She slammed my face onto the sheets, so my head was pressed awkwardly to the side.

She took a second length of rope, made a slipknot noose of it and circled the noose around my neck.

Then, throwing that rope across the width of the bed, Fulana stepped around to the other side and pulled the rope roughly so that the noose was frighteningly tight around my throat.

She attached the rope to the creaky bedsprings, leaving me uncomfortably gasping for breath and as securely pinioned to that ugly bed as I had ever been bound in my life.

I heard the soles of her big bare feet slapping the concrete floor as she returned to the dresser.

I knew what she was doing. She was fetching my wondrous rattan cane.

What a work of delight is the rattan cane. For centuries it has been wielded by sadistic schoolmasters on the exposed butts of errant schoolboys. The opportunity to beat scholarly bottoms can be a more potent incentive for one of sadistic bent than any monetary remuneration for the would-be teacher. Inherent sadism is a major incentive for cruel men to enter the profession of teaching.

With my head pressed against the bed's surface, I could not observe the expression on Fulana's face as she approached my bare exposed back and ass. But I summoned up visions of cruel glee illuminating her unlovely face.

I could hardly wait for her to begin.

But Fulana hesitated, taking pleasure at the discomfort she undoubtedly knew I felt in anticipation of the painful blows she would soon deliver to my tender naked skin.

She landed her first blow square across the middle of my buns. It was a masterful stroke. Solid, firm and impassioned. The thwack was a physical manifestation of the hatred, disgust and contempt she felt for the creepy *Norteamericano* who had flown down to her village to get his ass walloped.

It was glorious.

Her second swipe landed directly upon the welt raised by her first smack.

Yikes!

I could tell that this woman had mercilessly beaten recalcitrant burros, disobedient dogs and bothersome children into cringing submission to her will again and again. I had an expert disciplinarian venting a boiling fury upon my despicable being.

What could be more perfect?

I rewarded Fulana by giving full satisfying expression to sobs, screams, moans, tears and curses.

She broke her previous silence by shouting reviling terms at me. I did not understand the meaning of the words. But I caught the import: *hijo de la chingada, cabrón, pendejo, pinche hijo de tu puta madre, que chinga tu pinche madre...*

And this string of abuses coordinated rhythmically with the caning she was delivering to my back, ass, thighs, head, neck, hands, arms shoulders...

The woman was tireless. She certainly expended more physical torment than could be expected for the measly twenty dollars I was paying her.

With the noose around my neck, I did not have great latitude of motion. But there was just enough slack in the rope so I could hump the edge of the bed, back and forth...back and forth.

The combination of the severe beating I was receiving and the coordinated friction of my engorged dong against the sheets caused me to shriek at the top of my lungs as I came powerfully all over the sheet beneath me.

My orgasm appeared to irritate my torturer for she unleashed renewed fury upon my blistered, burning agonizing raw skin.

Oh, the rapture! The pain! The unspeakable delight!

No one on earth can possibly know the sensual delights known to us devoted masochists.

I believe I passed out from the pain at some point. At least, I cannot recall when the blows ceased and the sadistic bitch untied the end of the rope that was secured to the bedsprings.

I found myself in somewhat of a daze when I realized I was being led by my noose into the bathroom.

But, I was aware enough to feel the coolness of the concrete floor as I slumped down onto it.

As I lay there with my hands still bound behind me, my back ablaze from the savage beating I had received, and the feeling of relief in my balls from my giant orgasm, I looked up at the obese woman squatting over me.

Oh, boy! It was time for the grand finale.

Fulana slid her body back and forth above mine and peed and shit all over me, smearing her waste from my head to my heels.

When she finished her job, she went to the toilet, wiped her ass and cunt with the newspaper rectangles that served as toilet paper in that hotel and left me, bound, defiled and convulsing on the bare concrete.

No one can know how much I loved that woman at the time. I was eternally grateful to her. I adored her. She was my goddess.

She was Venus.

I struggled for well over an hour to free my wrists from their restraints. To no avail.

Eventually, Chuy came sauntering into the room wielding a butcher knife. He scornfully spit out the word *pendejo* at me, severed the rope binding my wrists together, laughed cruelly, and left me squirming in my filthy squalor.

How I loved vacationing in Zihuatanejo.

Now where, you might ask, did I pick up this novel form of sexual satisfaction?

I have already told you that masochism was a strand in the DNA I acquired at conception.

While that fact is true enough, the quality was certainly enhanced at home in my childhood.

I was raised by Mommy Dearest, a single mother who hated (and still hates) all men and boys

After her boyfriend Jack knocked her up, the bastard jilted her. You know, "It's been loads of fun, dear. A gossamer dream, and all that. But I'm outta here."?

The product of that fizzled romance was none other than...*Ta-da!*... yours truly.

And I was a great burden to Mommy Dearest. How do I know? Simple. She informed me so on a daily basis until I escaped from her loving care when I was old enough to bolt.

When I was six years old, Mommy Dearest (M.D.) brought home a good friend. A bull dyke who hated the male sex with a vehemence that surpassed that of M.D.

"Auntie" Gertrude, the ferocious lesbian, lived in our happy home and, along with M.D. served *in loco parentis.*

I got regular beatings from either or both of the vixens for infraction after infraction of previously undisclosed rules of the house.

Not that I minded getting my ass tanned. Truth to tell, I purposely committed such infractions as farting at the dinner table, wetting my bed, tracking lawn fertilizer (shit to you) into the house on my shoes, and, oh yes, sassing back.

My favorite provocation for punishment, though, came with the advent of puberty.

When I discovered jacking off, one or the other of the two viragos kept catching me at it.

How very puritanically furious those babes would get when they spied me doing that nasty male thing to my adolescent peter.

If I couldn't set the stage for one or both of them to catch me *in flagrante delicto*, I would jerk off into a handkerchief or into my underwear and drop the besmirched article into the clothes hamper. Or, there was always an opportunity to splotch jism in a viscous pool on my sheets.

So, before long, I began to associate beatings with orgasm.

The connection was bound to occur to me eventually anyway. But the dynamics of my loving home helped make the tie-in of pain-rapture at a crucial time in my life.

Auntie Gertrude was what I would call today a religious freak. She justified her lesbian proclivities by references to Holy Writ. She believed the Bible to be quite clear in stating that Delilah was a lesbian and that she was obeying God's dictate when she punished Samson for being what she called a male chauvinist pig. She saw Eve herself as the first lesbian ever who sought the fruit of the Tree of the Knowledge of Good and Evil so women could escape from the sexism that Adam represented.

Chapter by chapter and book by book, Auntie had a ready exegesis to prove that God hated the male sex and created a female version of our race to keep that poor sap Adam in his place.

I myself was never much into religion back when I lived with Mommy Dearest and Auntie. So I did not pay much attention to their religiosity.

Other than what I learned about martyrs.

It was Mommy Dearest who brought me a thick book full of tales about the Christian martyrs. She believed, and Auntie agreed, that if I read the vivid stories about those saintly masochists, it might just get me to mend my masturbatory ways.

That if I paid strict enough attention to the text of that pious book, I might actually see the light and stop flogging the bishop.

Oh how I loved the stories in that book. They sent me into raptures. I particularly enjoyed whacking off to those titillating tales. I always got a ball-stirring glow from stories about how those saints were so keen on being barbecued on gridirons. Or being boiled alive in hot oil or water. I got tingles reading about the guy who got off on being shot full of arrows. Then there were the freaks who proclaimed some kind of religious nonsense so they could be publicly applauded when they were thrown naked to the lions. I caressed myself to a high pitch when I read about the ones who got themselves torn limb from limb on the rack or wheel. And I was sure I would have volunteered to take the place of any of those pain-fetishists who got themselves nailed to crosses.

On my own, I got hold of a wonderful book about the Spanish Inquisition. Oh, what exquisite instruments those priests had on hand to burn, gouge, hack and drown the infidel martyrs. Such lovely torture. Enough to make anyone like me into an infidel martyr so he could experience such sophisticated torture.

There were so many different kinds of neat folks who suffered all that ravishing pain for their religion or for their infidelity to the "true faith." I would love to suffer for my own cult of SEX. I yearned to agonize to express my veneration of a cruel faithless woman who would be willing to punish me for being such a miserable wretched sinner. A Venus in leather.

From reading those two books, I made up a name for my strange and wonderful condition. I decided that what I exulted in was a "martyr complex." All the great martyred Christian saints and Spanish heretics clearly found bliss in their exquisite suffering. The more barbaric and frightful the torture, the more they enjoyed it.

Why, even today there are loads of Christians and Moslems who beat their own backs with whips. And how about those Buddhist monks who set themselves on fire? There are so many people of all faiths who suffer still other kinds of pain in order to enjoy spiritual sexual ecstasy.

Thank you Mommy Dearest! Thank you Auntie Gertrude! I owe you for enhancing my sex life at its very inception.

Because of the social dynamics of my home life, I tended to be a bit afraid of girls when I was in my early teens.

Oh, not that I was or am a faggot. I am in awe of females and their power over me. They are my goddesses. My Venuses in leather.

When I turned eighteen, I began to meet girls at bars. And I got lucky often enough. But I could not manage to get a single one of my dates to spank me. What was wrong with those women who agreed to accompany me into cheap motel rooms?

I finally wised up. I learned to recognize which girls in the bars were hookers. And I hit pay dirt there because word quickly spread among the Cyprians that there was a geeky lad in the neighborhood who would actually pay good money to get himself bound and beaten up. The girls used to vie for my business.

I worked flipping burgers at a fast-food joint at night for a while after I graduated from high school to get a little cash in my pockets. But my measly earnings only allowed me to support my BDSM fetish with the hookers once or twice a month.

Then I received a scholarship to the library science department at Dewey College in Claremont.

My Aunt Sarah lived in Claremont. Unlike Auntie Gertrude, Sarah was my genuine aunt, my mother's older sister. She was, well, still is, a sophisticated lady. The kind who holds salons, is part of the horsy set and is well-read. She is unlike my mother in so many ways. But she is very much like her in one respect. She has the same wonderful sadistic soul.

I have her to thank for my scholarship. She is a member of a number of lay committees of the college and has influence with the scholarship committee. I have a good idea how she wangled it. My grades in high school were good enough. But it takes more than just good grades to get a full scholarship to a prestigious college like Dewey.

I am sure that what it took in my case was a nice dose of nepotism.

Aunt Sarah had always told me I was her favorite nephew. Which was not too odd. After all, I was and am her only nephew.

She did not care much for her sister – my mother. And she thought a great deal less of Auntie Gertrude.

"Auntie!" How she hated to hear me call my mother's partner "Auntie." And woe betide me if I ever called Sarah "Auntie." Or even "Aunt" for that matter. She would only allow me to call her Sarah.

I thought she was a neat aunt. And I always felt she really was fond of me. And I knew that she arranged to land me the scholarship in order to get me out of the house of her disliked sister and her sister's despicable significant other.

When I arrived at Claremont, arrangements had all been made for me. I had free room and board at Glasscock Hall. My tuition was fully covered in the department of library science. And I received a monthly stipend that allowed me enough spending money to take care of my minimal needs.

When I visited Sarah to thank her for her kindness to me, she met me at the door of her Victorian style mansion attired in leather clothing.

The effect on me was electric. I had dreamed of women in leather for years. I kept a strip of black leather on my bedside table to rub, sniff and run over my stiff prick every night when I went to bed. My dream of a Venus in leather had haunted my dreams since adolescence.

And there, standing in the doorway of her mansion, bidding me enter her home, was a living embodiment of my leather fetish.

When I entered the door, Sarah held out her hand to me as though to shake *my* hand. But, I looked directly into her eyes and I knew, with absolute certainty that Sarah did not desire to shake my hand at all. My firm instinct was to lift that hand of hers to my lips. And as I kissed that dainty hand I dropped to my knees.

As I did so I heard her murmur, "Welcome to the purple world, Leo."

I was unable to speak to her, for I was in a true state of bliss. Her beautiful little hand was so delicate so rounded, so dimpled and so sensuous. And its luminous color was alabaster white.

I remained on my knees before Sarah, fondling that hand. She responded by graciously extending the other hand down to me. I fondly embraced those hands; one at a time, then clasped them together so I could worship them both. I kissed and I licked them. I sucked the fingers. I ran my tongue across the palms.

I fantasized how glorious it would be if she would ever deign to masturbate me with those sensuous hands. I was aware that that neither could nor would ever happen. Only in a dream. But how I longed to dream that very libidinous reverie. I knew that when my meeting with her was over, I would and could rush off to some private place and jack off, imagining it was Sarah's divine hand riding up and down my stiff pole.

At length, Sarah lifted her hands. And as she did so I rose up off my knees to where I could look into her eyes.

Her view descended from my face down to my groin.

Her vision dwelt on the massive hardon that danced behind my fly.

"You are standing before me boldly with an erection, Leo," she said softly yet decisively.

"I know, Sarah," I admitted. "I am sorry. So sorry. It is quite indecent of me."

"Don't you believe you deserve punishment for such outright bawdiness and vulgarity?" she asked me. This time her tone had a touch of disdain in it.

"Mamma always used a hairbrush to spank me with when I was naughty," I told her.

"How very common and bourgeois," Sarah scoffed. "It is about what I would expect from my seedy sister."

I had no retort for that.

"Were I to condescend to administer chastisement to you, I would consider my riding crop to be a more suitable instrument than a…um… hairbrush."

I nodded my head as a sign of encouragement on the direction her thinking seemed to be going.

"I keep my crop in my den," she explained. "Would you care to see it?"

Oh, Boy! Would I ever, I thought.

But verbally I only said something boyishly stupid like "That would be nice."

She turned heel and walked away from me. I supposed that was an invitation for me to follow her.

So follow her I did. And when she opened the door to her den, I stepped in behind her with my heart palpitating so furiously I felt sure she must be able to hear the thuds.

Sarah haughtily ordered me to remove my jacket, shirt and undershirt. I desperately wanted her to tell me to remove my trousers as well. But I knew she would feel that to be extremely improper.

I was resigned to having my nude torso be all the target her riding crop would ever even consider.

She returned with her whip from a closet and flung the leather thong a few times into the empty space in the room. It had a lovely sharp snap to it. My boner had shrunk some since my love session with her hands. The sight of her right hand wielding the crop, the grace with which she flicked it and the snapping sound when the leather thong reached its apex were all enough to revive a grand gush of blood right to the crown of my Johnson.

"Get down on your knees, Leo, and beg me to whip you for your impolite priapic behavior in the foyer."

I did a pretty convincing bit of beseeching.

"All right, then, Leo," she agreed. "I will administer twenty lashes to your back. That may be sufficient to punish you for your infraction this time. Do stand straight and tall, shoulders back, head up and face the fireplace with your back to me."

I stood there as rigid and proud as a Marine recruit.

And Sarah beat the hell out of my back. I could not stifle my sobs and moans. I was in Heaven.

After the twenty lashes were duly administered, Sarah told me to get dressed again.

"I have seen your class schedule, Leo," she told me. "I observe that you do not have any classes on Wednesdays at two in the afternoon.

"I would be willing to receive you on that day and time whenever you feel the need to atone for the disgusting thoughts and actions in which you engage."

I dropped to my knees, kissed Sarah's feet, and thanked her and left the mansion to go "shake hands with the mayor."

Every Wednesday for the remainder of my stay in Claremont I paid a dutiful call on my aunt. I always had a world of sins to atone for.

And she was always gracious enough to grant compensatory welts to my back in response. And, equally important to me, she always condescended to allow me to worship her voluptuous hands.

Oh, those joyful college years.

But after graduation, when I got my job as an assistant librarian and learned what I could get for twenty bucks a shot in tropical Mexico, the world was my oyster. Except for one flaw. Like all real masochists, I wanted my bondage and whippings administered by someone I loved. But, someone other than my maiden aunt who loved me enough to gratify my needs by humiliating and beating me.

But who was, after all, still my aunt.

Which leads me to tell you about my expedition to Ixtapa-Zihuatanejo. For it was there in that tropical paradise that I first caught sight of Wanda, my goddess, my Venus in leather.

CHAPTER TWO

CIRCE

Although I stayed in a flea-bag hotel in Zihuatanejo, that did not mean that was where I whiled away my days.

Oh, no. I preferred to pass the time of day in the tony community of Ixtapa. To be more precise, in the swankiest, most luxurious and most expensive resort in the area. The Hotel Ixtapa Ruiz.

I fit right in with the fancy vacationers at the Ruiz. I purchased my expensive tropical attire at the haberdashery located right within the hotel. So I was right in style.

I sat hour after hour on the beach beneath one of the resort's palapas ordering and sipping beverages as I watched the fat American tourists splash about in the tepid ocean waters before me.

And, during the warmest hours of the day, I escaped the heat and glare of the tropical sunshine in the air-conditioned majestic Cuauhtémoc Bar of the hotel.

Seating choices at the Cuauhtémoc consist of barstools at the bar itself, lounging chairs at the tables, and rounded benches in the booths.

At two in the afternoon I was always to be found sitting a chair at my favorite table facing the entry door and a cluster of booths.

The bartender and waitress knew that I always ordered their most expensive cocktail, the Mosca Azul and that I tipped lavishly.

I believe I was their favorite customer.

Day after day I sat at my table, imbibing my blue colored cocktail, ogling the customers as they drifted into the saloon as I ruminated on the books I had brought with me to Mexico.

I spent many a happy hour sitting at my favorite table thinking about the porn novels I had recently read back in my room in Zihuatanejo.

Then, on one particularly memorable morning, I awoke with a strange premonition that my life was about to change.

With a sense of happy anticipation, I donned my fancy attire, actually primping myself up like some kind of fancy Don Quixote out to encounter the Dulcinea of his dreams.

I headed for Ixtapa with spritely step.

And that very afternoon, would you believe?

I knew with a certainty that Fate had led me to that specific place at that particular time.

There is no armor against Fate.

For it was on that very afternoon that I first caught sight of Venus.

I was enjoying thinking about a porn novel I had read the previous night. It was a BDSM first-person tale about a sadistic gentleman who had used ingenious stratagems to trap an innocent kindergarten teacher into submitting to bondage and beatings at his hand.

It was a dandy little book. And, as frequently happened, soon after I had read it in my hotel room, it propelled me down to the dark, unlit nearby beach where I sprawled out on the sand under a swaying palm and whacked off, imagining the pleasure that kindergarten teacher must have felt at being so brutally subjugated.

As I was sitting at my table at the Ruiz recalling a particularly vivid episode in the book which was stimulating the first tremors of a hardon in my groin, I observed *her* walking into the room.

The woman who had just entered was very fair skinned and blond haired. Her languid eyes appeared to be emerald green in color. She was strikingly beautiful, voluptuously figured and regally poised.

She was fashionably attired, of course. But with two striking deviations from the local norm in her wardrobe. She wore a black leather bolero jacket and a pair of high black boots with stiletto heels.

In Ixtapa one sees precious little leather clothing of any kind.

As a leather fetishist myself, those articles definitely caught my attention.

The newly arrived lady glided over to a booth directly within my line of sight.

The cocktail waitress rushed over and took her order.

While waiting for her order, the Venus in leather glanced around the room. Our eyes engaged, but only for a fleeting moment. And, although her eyes continued their tour about the room, mine remained focused fixedly on her.

I was entranced. Nay, more. I was in love.

For the entire next week, I was ensconced daily at my table in that barroom, facing the booth Venus had taken that first afternoon. And I was not disappointed. At two o'clock she consistently returned to the saloon, proceeded to the same booth as before, ordered the same drink, and as she scanned the room our eyes engaged with each other for but a fleeting moment.

As I gazed at her day after day, my mind, as before, pondered the stories I had recently read in my tawdry room at the Pancho Villa.

At times I enjoyed thinking about lurid tales dealing with extreme cruelties. For I had no doubt whatsoever that the Venus in leather, who was my living idol, was cruel.

While gazing on her, my mind dwelt on stories about sadists like Count Vlad Dracula of Transylvania, known as Vlad the Impaler. I got off on descriptions of how he skewered his guests by running pointed poles up through his squirming guests' assholes and out their mouths. He was said to have skewered up to ten live victims at a time, one on top the other on the same stake.

And I worked up juicy erections recalling what I had read about villainous Roman emperors like Nero and Caligula who delighted in thinking up ever more and more gruesome tortures every day back in the days of the Empire.

But as I devoured Venus with my eyes, I dwelt especially on my favorite hoard of stories about Libussa, Lucretia Borgia, Agnes of Hungary, Queen Margo, Isabeau, Sultana Roxolane, and the sadistic Russian Czarinas.

I envisioned each of those sweethearts decked out in black leather and looking exactly like the woman across from me.

On the day I worked up my courage to make contact with my Venus, I happened to be sitting at my table at the Cuauhtémoc pondering the story of Circe.

You remember the tale, don't you? It is in Homer's *Odyssey*. It is one of my favorite tales in classical literature. I cannot even begin to tell you how many times I have re-read that story. And consequently got off on it.

Circe was a gorgeous, sexy enchantress who lived on the lovely island of Aeaea. The Mediterranean Sea washed many a shipwrecked sailor up onto the shores of her isle.

Circe suggestively lured each shipwrecked sailor into her magnificently furnished cave, and thence into her enticing bed.

She fucked the brains out of the poor sailor boy, thereupon turning him into a pig.

She loved torturing the herd of sailor-pigs that ran oinking noisily all over the floor of her cave.

What a woman! Cruel and inventive, with a twisted sense of humor. The very idea of her always makes my balls tingle.

Ever since I first read the Odyssey as a teenager, I had searched in vain for my own Circe, who would favor me by turning me into one of her porkers.

And now, at last, I believed I had found her, sitting statuesquely right before my adoring eyes.

Back at my home in California I had a framed reproduction of Botticelli's famed painting of Circe hung prominently in my bedroom. The original is owned by the Hermitage Museum in Saint Petersburg. I would have sold my soul to own that masterpiece.

But a genuine original appeared to be sitting in the Cuauhtémoc Bar. For the Venus sitting only a few yards away from me was a dead ringer for the Circe portrayed by Botticelli.

After a week of indecision, I gathered up enough nerve to attempt to contact my Circe.

I beckoned one of the mozos over to my table and told him to inform the lady that I would be pleased to buy her a drink. I slipped him a handsome enough tip to assure that he would show proper enthusiasm for his task.

I watched with great interest as he approached her booth. Circe nodded to him as he reached her. She smiled when she heard his message and then looked across the room directly at me. A fleeting smile crossed her lips and then she addressed the mozo.

When he heard her reply he bowed to her and quickly returned to my table.

His English was heavily accented, but quite intelligible.

"The señora say she would accept Rum Zombie. But only if señor bring it to booth himself. Offer it to her on bend knees."

I thanked the fellow, added a trifle to the tip I had previously given him, and summoned the cocktail waitress.

I ordered a Rum Zombie which she brought to me beaming a lovely wide smile. I was sure she and the bartender had kept a close watch on the action and had pumped the mozo about the correspondence he had carried between the señor and the señora.

I picked up the Zombie and with solemn step carried it across the room to the booth where the object of my affections haughtily observed my progress.

I knelt down on the floor on both knees and proffered the libation up towards her.

She accepted it with a cold smile.

The cocktail lounge had something like twenty customers in it at the time. The sight of a geeky guy down on his knees holding a drink up to a distinguished lady must certainly have evoked some amused interest.

Did I care what others might think of my ridiculous posture? Not a whit.

My Circe took a sip of her drink and placed the glass down on the table before her.

From her expression I knew she expected me to remain on my knees. I would have been disappointed were that not so.

"I have been aware of you rudely staring at me for over a week. You apparently have the manners of a boor," she said witheringly.

She spoke perfect English, but with an accent. I later discovered that the accent was Dutch. Or, to be more specific, Surinamese Dutch. But more of that at another time.

"Boor, peasant or prince, Madame," I answered. "I wish to be whoever or whatever may please your fancy. All I seek is to know who you are."

"Just who do you think I am?" she asked with a smile that was close cousin to a sneer.

"Circe," I hazarded.

She burst out laughing.

"Circe!" she responded. "You mean that sorceress Homer wrote about?"

Wonderful! I thought. *Not only beautiful, but classically educated.*

"Sandro Botticelli painted a masterpiece, *Circe in her Cave...*" I began.

"I know. I know," she snapped at me. "It hangs in the Hermitage. I have personally seen it there."

An art lover! A world traveler! A sophisticate!

I thought my head would explode from sheer joy.

I shuffled my knees to get a bit more comfortable.

"Stay on your knees, Dork," she ordered. "Remain perfectly still and I will tell you what kind of Circe I am.

"My name actually is Wanda van Domme. I am a native of Surinam. But I dwell now temporarily in a town called La Jolla. It is in California. A community neighborhood of San Diego."

Oh fate! My own residence was in Ocean Beach, another San Diego community not far distant from La Jolla. What Zihuatanejo is to Ixtapa, Ocean Beach is to La Jolla.

She told me she came to La Jolla from Surinam on a whim to take post- graduate courses in English and American Literature at the University of California, San Diego (UCSD).

I told her my name, Leo Messick. And that I was an assistant librarian at a branch library in San Diego and lived in Ocean Beach.

Her scornful laugh told me everything I needed to know about what she felt about an assistant branch librarian who lived in Ocean Beach.

As I waited uncomfortably for what she might say next, she took a slow, satisfying sip of her cocktail, kept the potation in her mouth for a long while, and then swallowed it.

She then looked deeply into my eyes, silently, as though examining an amusing but insignificant insect.

She then returned to the discussion about Circe.

"So, Leo Messick of Ocean Beach," she mused. "Were you really thinking about Circe during that whole week while you were leering at me so boldly and lasciviously?"

Bold? Lascivious? Moi?

I countered, "You are a dead ringer for the model Botticelli used when he painted his masterpiece,"

She laughed.

"Because of the blond hair and green eyes?" she scoffed. "Then you could have found your Circe any time of the day or night in any of the northern European nations."

"No," I remonstrated. "The similarity between you and Botticelli's Circe goes way beyond pigments. The outstanding feature that links you with her is what your features express."

"And what might my features portray that label me as the sorceress Circe?" she demanded.

"Cruelty, Lady," I gushed. "Sybaritic cruelty. Mixed with haughty disdain and contempt. I have sought a lovely lady like you who displays such a countenance all my life. And from the moment I caught sight of you coming into this room, I was struck dumb."

"Are you trying to tell me you love this image you have of Circe?" she laughed.

"With all my heart," I affirmed.

"But are you not aware that if you choose to love Circe, she will surely turn you into a swine?"

"I am aware" I avowed.

"Into the swine you really have always wanted to be?" she continued.

"Into the swine I have always known myself to be," I agreed.

"And are you not further aware that she will treat you with severe cruelty?" Wanda pressed further.

"With *loving* cruelty," was my fervent answer.

Wanda laughed quite openly at that.

"Oh, Leo," she said through her laughter. "You truly amuse me. You are such a dork. But, I have to admit, you're a cute dork.

"Yet I have to warn you. I am irresistible to dorky nerds like you. So, beware!"

A silence hung heavily over us following her warning.

After a long, pregnant pause, Wanda said:

"Tell me honestly, Leo. What is it you really want? Dig down into the dark bowels of your soul and search diligently for an answer. And do not respond to my question until you are sure you have encountered the dreadful truth."

I did not have to dig very deep for my answer.

I told her, "All I want is to be the slave of a woman I worship."

She replied, "You mean a woman who will mistreat you because you worship her?"

"Yes," I affirmed. "One, who will bind me, whip me, humiliate me, scorn me and betray me. And yet," I added, "she will do all that because she loves me."

"Such a woman will certainly flaunt a rival lover before your fear-filled eyes," Wanda warned me. "And that rival will cruelly subject you to his sadistic whims before your mistress as she smiles and exults in your misery."

"For the sake of the goddess I seek, I would support even that," I told her.

"You seem to me to be a great simpleton, Leo," she told me. "Don't you know a real woman is fickle? She will love Tom today, Dick tomorrow and mess around with Harry whenever he's in town. You mention a goddess. Aren't you aware that Venus herself was never faithful to any of the gods or mortals she fucked? Are you sure you are up to dealing with of a real live goddess?"

As a response, I decided to tell her about my martyr complex.

"All the saints and mystics insist that their souls derive exquisite pleasure from the torments of the body," I explained. "True rapture can only be known by those who submit their egos to selfless humiliation and degradation.

"That, Wanda, is the martyrs' creed by which I live."

Circe's face clouded over with anger.

I wondered if she had even listened to my carefully thought out explication of my martyr complex. It turned out that she was consumed with wrath only because I had dared to utter her given name.

She slapped my face smartly with the back of her lovely hand.

"Worm," she spit out. "I have not given you leave to call me Wanda. Understand that I will not allow you to address me otherwise than as Circe until further notice. And I shall address you, in turn, with terms like Swine until I tell you otherwise."

I apologized profusely for having dared to call her Wanda, as I bent my lips down to kiss her boot.

That appeased her anger.

In a very serious vein, then, my newly discovered goddess told me she was a person who had a great need for toys.

I immediately fathomed her purpose in abruptly turning the subject of our discussion to toys.

My statements had caused her to consider that the worm groveling at her feet might just possibly be a candidate to become one of her playthings. She could tell by my expression that I understood what she was attempting to convey to me.

"You have to realize, Swine, that I pick toys up, use them, abuse them, then cast them off.

"I have given you fair warning. Beware. Anyone fool enough to fall in love with me and whom I decide to love in return is doomed. For such a fool becomes my personal toy. And I have a deep seated need for *lots* of toys."

I told her: "It sounds to me as if by 'toy' you actually mean 'slave'."

"Exactly, she agreed. "I must have slaves. An army of slaves if possible."

"And I, for my part, must have a domina to subject me," I answered. "For that, I would give anything."

"Even your freedom?" she asked with a cruel leer.

"Particularly my freedom," was my honest answer.

I lowered my upper body down onto the carpet and kissed her foot again.

"I have just told you my deepest dream," I avowed.

Circe reached down and encircled my neck with her soft, warm sensuous hands. I would have willingly submitted to being strangled on the spot by those divine hands.

She closed the grip on my neck menacingly.

I nearly swooned.

"My most fervent dream is to be the abject slave of a beautiful woman whom I love and worship," I affirmed.

"Even if she wantonly mistreats you?" she laughed.

"Yes," I declared. "One who cuffs me, whips me and tramples me underfoot even as she succumbs to another man's lust."

"Would you even submit to her cruelty should she give you to her lover who would ravage you sexually while she witnesses the act with glee?"

I told her that her suggestions far exceed anything I had ever dared imagine. That I now doubly desired to be her slave.

She haughtily informed me that she does not accept anyone as a slave until he demonstrates his suitability for the position.

"I have already told you, Swine, that I have observed that many of the candidates who seek the privilege of suffering the infliction of my whip show acceptable capacity to bear physical pain. It is only the few, the truly admissible, who have the quality of wallowing under harsh humiliation.

"You yourself must have both relished and undergone quite a few humiliating experiences or you would not have dared prostrate yourself at my feet. Tell me some of the disgusting things you have done recently in order to convince me you are contemptible enough to even interest me."

I told her about Fulana and how I had permitted her to shit all over me. Circe seemed pleased to hear how vile and odious I had been.

I related how I nightly read atrocious pornography in my wretched room in Zihuatanejo and then go out and publicly jack off by the seashore.

She liked my disclosure about Fulana's fecal mortification to my bound, naked body more than my milder practice of public (though deeply nocturnal) masturbation. But she agreed that I was, indeed, a pretty abominable wretch and richly deserved severe bondage and physical discipline.

"But, Piggy, Piggy," she declared. "Before I could condescend to bind and beat you, what have I said you need to do?"

"To endure humiliation at your hands, Circe," I uttered, grateful that she seemed to be even considering dominating me.

"I will allow you to prove your metal to me, then, tomorrow," she informed me.

With a surge of exuberance I blurted out, "Oh, Joy! I will willingly submit myself to the glory of mortification at your hands. For you are my goddess. My Venus."

I then went on to blurt:

"I see you as my Venus in Leather. And all I want is to be your votary and worship you!"

"For the present, forget Venus. For you, I am merely Circe, Fool," she scowled.

"Return to this saloon at this same time tomorrow. There will be a handsome blond Gringo named Blake sitting at this booth at two in the afternoon. You must approach him and convince him to follow you to my room in this hotel. It is room six, six, six.

"You have to get him to enter the room.

"And once the two of you are there, you will have to stand there and observe whatever the man and I are doing before your very eyes. And you must bear it with equanimity.

"Following your gawking, you will have to submit to whatever Blake does to you as he humiliates you while I look on.

"For now, though, Porky, stay sprawled there on the floor where you are and do not dare arise until I have left the room."

Circe remained seated and slowly finished drinking her Zombie.

When she finished her drink, she arose, stepped over me, and lustily gave me a hefty kick to the ribs with the pointed toe of her right boot.

I heard gasps of surprise from other customers in the Cuauhtémoc as Wanda exited the room.

I arose from the floor grasping my painful ribcage, and staggered to the door under the scornful gaze of everyone in the room.

As I exited the lounge, I was smiling widely and contentedly.

She said I was a cute dork. *She must love me.*

I think she really loves me.

I got very little sleep that night. Back in my dreary room at the Pancho Villa I could not even relieve the long wakeful hours by reading *Teaching the Milkmaid to Suck* or any of the other porn novels I had brought to read during my Mexico vacation.

Instead, I went out and wandered around La Madera Beach under the full romantic tropical moon, doing nothing more than playing gently with my dick and fantasizing about Wanda.

In my reveries I dared call her Wanda from time to time, slapping my prick for my impertinence. At other times I romantically called her Circe and gave spit-lubricated caresses to my peckerhead as I did so. And yet, other times, I adoringly called out to her in a languid whisper, "Venus!," as I jacked off against a swaying palm tree.

At about six o'clock in the morning the moon set into the murmuring Pacific and I was heavy-eyed enough to need some sleep.

I went to a restaurant frequented by the local fishermen and had myself a breakfast of *menudo, pan dulce* and *café con leche.*

I was back in my room a bit before seven. I flopped into bed and fell asleep with my prick encircled by my loving right hand.

I slept deeply and did not awake until eleven when a criado came bumbling into my room to hose it down as he did every morning.

Once he had fully awakened me, I was all smiles, remembering this was the day Wanda van Domme was going to give me the opportunity to prove I was worthy of being her slave.

At noon I arrived at the Ruiz in fine fettle. Before I went there, I had gone to a barbershop in Zihuatanejo and gotten a shave and a haircut. I had the barber give a lavish application of Bay Rum to my healthily glowing skin. I was dressed in a beautifully starched white guayabera shirt and gleaming white linen trousers.

What a magnificent sight I was.

The Ixtapa Ruiz has an outside luncheon patio where I had a perfectly prepared plate of *huachinango a la veracruzana* accompanied by a tropical fruit salad.

I was wrapped in a cloud of joy in anticipation of how well I would soon be pleasing my goddess by displaying my absolute subjection to her cruel will.

I arrived at the Cuauhtémoc Bar at one-thirty. I felt it was important to display how anally retentive I was, in case Wanda or that Blake guy, whoever he was, should look in to check up on me.

At two o'clock I had been sitting at my table sipping moscas azules long enough to feel the courage I had imbibed with the booze.

My eyes were focused on the door. When would that fellow, Blake, make his appearance?

Two o'clock. Two ten. Two seventeen. Two twenty-two.

How the minutes dragged on.

Where *was* that dude?

Would he really come? Was Wanda playing a hoax on me? Was this waiting game an example to me of how she played piteously with her toys?

Two twenty-three.

Aha!

A strapping blondish dude swaggered into the room He made no attempt to check out whether anyone might be expecting him and sauntered over to the booth Wanda had occupied the previous afternoon.

The waitress went to take his order.

In a loud arrogant voice he ordered a Dos Equis.

When the beer was brought to his booth, he took a deep gulp, belched and laughed.

I decided that if that jerk was Blake, I did not much care for him.

Well, like him or not, I girded up my loins, got up from my table and approached his booth.

I stood beside him and cleared my throat.

He totally ignored me, took another swig of his beer and belched loudly again.

What a boor. A real "ugly American."

"Excuse me, Sir," I said.

He glowered at me.

"What the Hell do *you* want, Creep?" he growled.

"Do you happen to be Blake?" I asked.

"Maybe I am. Maybe I ain't," he shot back belligerently. "What's it to you?"

"If you *are* Blake," I told him. "I am a friend of Wanda van Domme. She told me to meet you here."

"Wanda didn't tell me to expect no candy ass like you, Junior," he grunted. "Scram, Asshole."

"I really need to speak to you," I whined.

"I said 'get lost.' Are you deaf or just plain stupid?" he snarled.

I did not know what to do. I could not continue to stand there as the dolt continued to insult me. People were beginning to stare. No doubt many of them had observed me the previous afternoon as I was groveling down on my knees next to that same booth.

That was bad enough. But this was *really* embarrassing.

So I did the only thing I could do. I sat down at the booth across the table from that impolite Gringo.

"Look, Shit Ass," Blake grumbled. "No one invited you to sit there. Are you looking for me to give you a knuckle sandwich or what?"

"Look, Blake," I said entreatingly. "I know who you are. And I know you know Wanda van Domme. And I urgently need you to accompany me to her room."

He finished his beer as I sat there patiently waiting for him to answer me.

He belched across the table into my face.

"Buy me two beers, Fuck Face," he ordered.

Well, great! Now we were getting somewhere.

I beckoned to the waitress and ordered two beers for Blake and paid the tab as it then stood for the two of us.

When the waitress brought the lout his order, he glared at me.

"Now, Asshole," he grunted. "You just sit there keeping your yap shut while I enjoy my brews in peace. I don't want to hear a fucking peep out of you until I've slacked my thirst.

"While I am so engaged, I want you to think about what it's worth to you for me to "accompany you" to some room or other."

I sat quietly as the rude fellow slowly drank and belched. It seemed to take him forever.

He did not acknowledge in any way that I was sitting there as he savored his brews.

He finally took the last swallow of his drinks.

"Well?" he said as he wiped the foam off his lips with the back of his hand.

I did not know how to answer him.

"You just gonna sit there looking stupid, Idiot?" he asked arrogantly.

I gulped.

"Didn't I ask you a while back what it's worth to you for me to help you out?" he growled.

That wasn't exactly what he'd asked. But I was not about to argue.

"I suppose I could pay you something," I stammered.

"How much in American dollars is in it for me to take you to the room of this dame you're talkin' about? I'm not some kind of goddam pimp, you know. So I don't wanna hear nothing less than five hundred dollars outta you."

Five hundred dollars! For him just accompany me to Wanda's room? That's atrocious. I was getting taken for a patsy by this thug. But what could I do?

"I don't have five hundred dollars on me," I complained.

"Then get lost," he scoffed. "Come back when you've got five hundred dollars. Good bye, Chump."

"How about an I.O.U.?" I asked hopefully.

"I said, 'Get lost,'" he reiterated.

"I can get five hundred dollars in pesos at the bank," I ventured.

He appeared to think that over.

"Tell you what," he said in a more reasonable tone than he had used before.

"You come back here tomorrow at this same time with all them pesos and we'll talk. O.K.? Now scram!"

I slunk out of that bar, totally mortified.

I would have no problem getting the requisite pesos using my credit card at the Banco de México branch I did business with in Zihuatanejo. That was not really the problem.

The problem wasn't even that I felt I was being taken advantage of by that despicable fellow American.

What really hurt was that I had been primed to see Wanda that afternoon and show her how beautifully I could submit to her humiliation.

But, as I thought things over I cheered up.

I had just been rudely humiliated by Blake. And I believed I had shown that I could deal with humiliation quite abjectly. I felt that Wanda would be pleased at how submissively I had behaved.

I was pretty proud of myself.

From Ixtapa I went directly to my bank in Zihuatanejo. Using my credit card to access five hundred dollars, I exchanged them for seven thousand pesos.

I tucked the massive stack of bills into an envelope the clerk at the bank gave me and treaded my gloomy path back to the Pancho Villa.

I would have to while away about twenty tedious hours before I could meet that obnoxious jerk, Blake, again, back at the bar.

I contemplated a session with Fulana, but decided that was not a helpful course at the time.

Or I could return to Ixtapa and get stinko on moscas azules.

No, I decided. *Counterproductive.*

A third thought I had was to go down to La Madera Beach, sit down under a palapa and drink myself silly while gazing at the blue waters of the Pacific.

No. I would get sick and tired of that pretty rapidly.

However, I further considered, if, when I went down to the beach, I took along enough porn reading to keep me in a high priapic state hour after hour, and if I wore my swimming trunks, I could check out whether it was possible to get my rocks off into the ocean when I waded out into the tepid water up to my bellybutton and wanked off.

(And, yes, Folks. If you really want to know. If you play with your whang in those warm tropical waters, you can, indeed, augment the sea with streams of your own jism.)

The next day, I arrived back at the bar of the Ruiz bearing my envelope full of pesos and my heart replete with hope.

As on the previous afternoon, I had arrived at the bar way early.

Wouldn't a domina want her prospective slave to prove he was an anal retentive?

I stoked my courage with liberal doses of my favorite cocktail.

And some twenty minutes or so after two, in strutted the unbearable prick who had put me through my paces just twenty-four hours previously.

I waited until he had settled into his booth. He ordered his two beers and loudly announced, "Put these on Cunt-face's tab. And add on a fifty percent tip for yourself, Sweetie Pie."

Whether or not the Mexican waitress caught the full coarseness of this *vaurien's* orders, I could not tell. For she showed no shock or displeasure and simply proceeded to the bar to fill the order.

But most of the customers in the room were Gringos, and they appeared to me to draw a collective gasp at the churl's vulgarity.

I waited until he was served before rising from my table and joining him at his booth.

I was absolutely mortified as I sensed the eyes of everyone in the room following my progress across the room.

I sat at the booth without waiting for an invitation.

"Yeah?" Blake addressed me. "Where's the dough?"

I handed him the envelope, which was bulging with peso notes.

He did not deign to look inside the envelope. He knew I would not dare welch on him by so much as a centavo.

Blake did not address me further. He slowly slurped downed his beers, signaled to the waitress to bring the tab and coolly observed me pay for his drinks and my own.

"O.K., Asshole," he said as the waitress retreated back to the bar.

"It's your goddam call. Where do you wanna go now?"

"Room six, six, six," I told him.

He laughed derisively as he got up from the booth.

"Room six, six, six? O.K., Chump. If that's what you want, it's *your* funeral. Follow me."

He led me to a bank of elevators, pushed a button and lurched into a car as its door slid open.

I followed him into it wondering what he had meant by "it's your funeral."

When the cabin arrived at the sixth floor, I followed him out the door and into the luxurious hallway.

When we got to the door of Wanda's room, Blake said to me, "Here we are, Sap. See ya'." And he started to head back towards the elevator.

"No, wait!" I called out. "I need you to come into the room with me."

He looked back at me over his shoulder.

"Our agreement didn't have nothin' in it about me goin' into no room, Chum. Forget about it," was his brusque reply.

I protested that it was essential for me to get him into the room.

He stopped, turned around and headed back towards me.

"There's gotta be somethin' in it for me, ya' know," he insisted.

"What do you want now?" I asked with a sinking feeling in my stomach.

"Hand me your wallet," he demanded as he stepped up in front of me.

I felt I had no choice and handed my billfold over to the scoundrel.

He looked inside and pulled all the bills out.

I know I had about a thousand pesos in there.

"This'll have to do," he smirked, putting the bills in his pocket.

"Go ahead, Pal. Knock on the door. Let's go see the little lady."

With a mixture of pleasant anticipation and a bit of trepidation I knocked on the door.

Wanda did not answer my knock immediately. Nor did I expect her to. A goddess does not flit about with unseemly haste.

I stood tall and erect directly in front of the door. That rascally Blake stood firmly behind me.

At length a silvery voice penetrated the wooden door.

"Who is there?"

Oh, that voice. Sweet, yet imperious. Clear, yet accented.

The very sound sent shock waves through my groin.

"Leo," I answered back. "It's Leo Messick, Wanda. The man from the Cuauhtémoc Bar you invited to see you."

"I am quite sorry," came a crisp reply. "I fear I am not acquainted with anyone of that name. Please go away. And do not annoy me further."

Doesn't know anyone...?

Of course. How stupid of me.

"I beg your pardon, Circe," I called back. "It is I, Swine. I beg your pardon for forgetting your instructions to me."

"Oh, yes, Swine," she responded. "Have you come alone or are you accompanied by someone?"

"Blake kindly agreed to join me here. He is standing right behind me," I informed her.

The door opened. And, Oh Heavens! What a sight met my eyes!

There stood Circe. Nay, more than Circe. For the goddess who radiated her presence in the entryway of the room was attired in a leather cat suit. She wore a pair of high, black platform boots with stiletto heels and a leather domina cap. One of her hands was on her left hip and a cat-o'-nine tails was gripped in her right hand.

The vision was beyond my most fervent imaginings. Framed by the open door was my Venus in leather. A vision. An icon. A living goddess.

I stood there for a while utterly stunned.

Suddenly, Blake gave me a rough shove from behind, sending me stumbling headlong into the room aimed directly at my goddess.

Wanda/Circe/Venus stepped deftly aside and I fell flat on my face on the floor beside her.

"Clumsy prick," Blake announced as he stepped into the room and closed the door behind him.

I was seething with anger at the blackguard who had purposely created a buffoonery of my hoped-for dignified entrance to the Temple of Venus.

But rather than vent my anger at the lout I converted my sprawl into a crawl and kissed the boot of my goddess.

"Venus," I declared. "I am here."

The strands of her whip cut across my back.

"Not Venus to you, yet, Swine," she spat out. "You have barely yet risen to a level where you may address me as Circe."

How stupid of me. I had been overcome by the vision I had seen when the door opened.

I had to remember. *Circe.* I would have to earn the right to call her Venus. My Venus in Leather.

I was too close to her when she had slashed me with her whip for it to cut through my guayabera shirt. As a matter of fact, the impact had been devoid of pain. I interpreted it as a love-tap.

My curious eyes scanned her suite.

It consisted of three rooms – living room, bedroom and bathroom.

The décor and furnishings were elegant Mexican Colonial. In very good taste. Very chic,

Wanda walked over to a taboret, laid her whip on it and picked up a dog collar and leash.

She returned to where I was crouching, put the collar about my neck and attached the leash.

She handed the end of the leash to Blake.

"Here, Dearie," she said. "Walk piggy boy as he crawls on his hands and knees. You know where to take him."

She then addressed me:

"And you, Piggy. Look up at Master Blake. Smile gratefully and say "Oink!" to tell him how much you appreciate all that he is doing for you"

Now *that* was really difficult. Blake's treatment of me up to that point had been execrable. When I looked up into his face he was sending me an insolent sneer.

But this was my first real opportunity to demonstrate to my mistress that I really could be submissive to her will. She surely knew that I had to detest the cad at the other end of the leash.

So, smile I did. And "oink" I did.

And for my efforts Blake gave me a good hard yank on the leash that felt like it would pull my neck bones right out of joint.

I crawled forward as rapidly as my hands and knees would carry me so as to keep some slack on the leash between Blake and me. It seemed to me he purposely kept hastening his pace to re-gain the tension.

When Blake and I got to the bedroom, Wanda was already there.

She took the leash from Blake's hand and bent down to unsnap it from my collar.

After giving her an adoring smile I looked around the room.

It was furnished and adorned like the living room in Mexican Colonial style.

The most notable and magnificent furnishing was the heavy four-poster bed.

The posts were made of massive columns of a dark brown wood. The carvings on it were of Aztec or Toltec design. They were magnificent works of art.

Wanda told me to remove my clothing, fold it carefully and stack it in the corner.

She and Blake sat on the edge of the bed watching me disrobe. I found their attention to me rather disconcerting.

Once I was embarrassingly naked, my mistress said:

"That was nicely done Bowser. So I am going to reward you."

Bowser?

"For the moment, I am promoting you from being a pig to that of obedient canine."

That would explain "Bowser."

"As for myself," she continued. "I am bored to death with being Circe. I find the role tiresome. I must warn you, Bowser, that I am quite changeable, even fickle, in my moods and in the roles I play.

"Today, I am Diana, the goddess of the hunt. You are Bowser, one of my pack of hunting dogs. And, let it be noted, not necessarily yet the lead hound.

"The youth sitting beside me is Endymion, my would-be lover.

"I am a chaste goddess, so Endymion is forbidden to make love to me. But, chaste as I am, I love his body and take pleasure in caressing it.

"So sit on your haunches where you are, Cur, and observe. I will inform you further what to do when Endymion and I are in costume.

"Arise, Endymion," she ordered. "I must prepare you for your part in the next act."

Blake got up, glanced at me and snarled. Apparently my goddess's games were not totally alien to him.

Damn his soul

While I watched, Diana removed Blake's clothing slowly, seductively, piece by piece, until he stood before her naked, as Endymion, her lover who was forbidden to touch her.

I got some satisfaction out of that.

I had to admit the scoundrel had a splendid physique. No doubt the result of spending dollars and hours in some damned gym or other.

He had only nature to thank for the fact that he was marvelously hung.

Damn!

Diana stood between Endymion and Bowser (me) and gracefully and enticingly removed her own leather adornments.

The effect was to arouse simultaneous hardons on the part of her two subservients.

Because, at this point in my acquaintance with my goddess I suddenly became aware that Blake was not Wanda's lover any more than I was. He was merely one of her subservients, playing out a role in the dramas his domina created spontaneously. Whether he was a full-fledged slave at the time, or merely, like me, one who was attempting to prove he was worthy of the honor, I could not possibly even guess.

What a divine goddess Diana was.

Her blonde tresses cascaded over her shoulders, encircling her voluptuous alabaster-hued breasts with their "fair musk-rose" shaded nipples. Her blonde tufted mons veneris which led the eye down to her pouty-lipped mound fairly intoxicated me.

My hungering eyes cast their glances at her enchantingly turned ankles. A sight which caused my scrotum to clench.

What can I say. The live Diana before me surpassed even the dream that must have inspired Richard MacDonald to create that precious statue of the Moon Goddess of his.

John Keats' immortal poem, Endymion, played through my mind as my Diana arranged *her* Endymion's body on the massive bed in the state of sweet repose envisioned by the poet.

A thing of beauty is a joy forever/Its loveliness increases; it will never/ Pass into nothingness; but still will keep/A bower quiet for us, and a sleep/ Full of sweet dreams, and health, and quiet breathing.

As in that famed poem, Endymion, lying outstretched, nude, received the silvery caresses of the goddess. And, by Diana's will, he was doomed to know the ecstasy of her touch while having to restrain himself from any outward response in return for her caresses.

My Diana hovered over the virile muscled body of her luxuriously exposed, dormant-appearing Endymion. She traced her fingers lightly through his hair. Then, one hand remaining atop his head, the fingers of her other hand traced gossamer patterns over his lips and chin.

Both hands now played at making sensuous patterns over his nipples, across his abdomen, and down along his thighs.

This was the most intense torture I believe I had ever endured up to that time. I knew I was forbidden to play with my own body in response to the games Diana exercised on her Endymion. But I was overwhelmed with temptation.

Hands! Keep your distance from my boner.

Although she had forbidden Endymion (and by inference me) from any outward response, our male members were not capable of repose.

Two throbbing dicks pulsated in the scented air.

As she inserted a finger into Endymion's mouth, the fingers of Diana's other hand were drawing arabesques around his balls. As she inserted her tongue into Endymion's mouth, her loosely clasping fist was riding slowly up and down his extended trembling staff.

There was no question in my mind that my enemy, Blake, was suffering agonies in his bodily restraint. And I, a forced observer, finally could not keep my hand off my own peter. I had resisted to the extent of my abilities. But I simply had to caress my boner.

There I sat on my haunches, jacking off openly as I watched the Moon Goddess making love to her beloved shepherd.

Blake was showing himself a better slave than I. His hands remained resting on the surface of the bed as his goddess drove him to obvious absolute mad distraction.

Quite suddenly, Diana removed her hands from her victim's body and stepped away from the bed.

She looked directly at me and caught me *in flagrante delicto.*

"Up on your hind legs, Bowser," she ordered

I bounced up, but was unable to unclench my hand from my over-stimulated cock immediately.

"Come here, Endymion!" she ordered her previous victim.

Blake was at her side in a trice. I saw that his pecker was as engorged as mine. I was not sure which of us was the more pitiful martyr. Yet, I knew we were each very willing martyrs to Diana's merciless torment.

My goddess produced several strands of rope from a bedside stand and bade Endymion bind me hand and foot, spread-eagled, to the elaborate bedposts

He clearly took glee in stretching me as tightly and as painfully as possible. He must have learned to inflict sadistic bondage somewhere. I suspected it was my Wanda who had previously instructed him.

Without allowing him to relieve the tension to his cock and balls, Wanda made Blake dress himself while I remained bound to the bedposts awaiting what I knew would be a severe whipping. My Love put her cat suit back on and became, again, Circe.

She had brought her cat-o'-nine-tails into the bedroom.

In a clear, cool, cruel voice, she addressed the erstwhile Endymion who was now reduced to being a mere "Blake."

"Here, Sweetheart," she said. "Take this whip and reduce that wretch tied to the bedposts to a bloody-backed howling beaten dog. He seeks pain. Let's see how he manages it."

That muscled brute wielded Circe's whip with a mighty vengeance. He rained blow upon blow upon my back. I could not stifle the screams, cries, sobs, and groans that issued unbidden from within the recesses of my soul.

The unpleasant fact that it was my enemy who inflicted the blows was outweighed by the knowledge that my goddess was witnessing my suffering. And that, after all, was what I truly yearned for.

At length, Blake's exhaustion rather than the damage to my epidermis brought the flaying scourge to an end.

It was Circe's loving hands that released the ropes that bound me to the bedposts.

I thanked her with the few vocal resources I still had access to.

"Go get yourself dressed," she ordered me.

When I was fully clothed, she handed me a piece of note paper.

"When you return to San Diego, telephone me at this number if you still wish to subjugate yourself totally to my domination," she told me.

"You have proved yourself worthy of being a candidate for slavery.

"But, as long as you remain in Mexico, I forbid you to return to Ixtapa in any attempt to see me. Farewell until I return to San Diego."

And that was, indeed, the last time I saw her until we had both returned to the States.

As to that bastard Blake…I never, ever, saw the son of a bitch again.

CHAPTER THREE

BLESSED SERVITUDE

As soon as I arrived home in San Diego after my Mexico vacation I telephoned the number Wanda had given me.

There was no response from an answering machine, a voice mail, or a call forwarding.

There was no answer at all.

Just an infernally frustrating series of annoying rings.

I called at least ten times every day, to no avail.

Each time I let the phone ring twenty, thirty, forty times.

I relieved my frustration by jacking off to the sound of those annoying staccatos of buzz, buzz, buzz…

That "self-abuse" helped relieve my anxiety, sexual tension and boredom.

I wished Wanda had told me back in Ixtapa when she planned to return to San Diego. But I realized that a goddess does not deign to reveal details about her comings and goings to her subservients. A true devotee must learn the virtue of patience.

After about three weeks of daily anguish on my part I dialed and got an answer. It was a simple "Hello." But the mere sound of Wanda's silvery voice sent shudders of pleasure throughout my body.

I answered impulsively.

"Hello, Wanda? It's me. Leo. How are you?"

Her answer was a monosyllable.

"Who?"

Oh my God! After that long wait to get through to her, I had messed up. I had addressed her as Wanda and identified myself as Leo. Stupid, stupid, stupid!

I nearly hung up in order to try again to make a more appropriately telephonic entrance. But after having attempted to get through to her unsuccessfully for weeks, I dared not lose her now.

"Sorry," I blurted. "I mean, it's me, Swine."

Or was I supposed to be Bowser? Try again.

"That is to say, Bowser" I rapidly corrected myself.

"Oh, yes, Bowser," she said as though attempting to call back a mental picture of someone she might have met casually once. "What do you want?"

Good gracious! What did I want? I want to worship you. I want you to beat me. I want...

"When I last saw you, in Ixtapa," I told her, you gave me a piece of paper."

"Really?" she asked, as though trying to recall the occasion.

"Yes," I answered. "Really. And on that paper you wrote that I had proved myself worthy of becoming a candidate for slavery. And you invited me to call you at this number if I wished to subject myself totally to your domination."

"Did I really?" she asked, as if surprised.

"Oh, yes, Circe," I swore. "You did. I am holding that precious paper right now next to my heart as we speak."

"I do seem to recall something of that nature," she replied. "You were the dork whom Blake beat with such relish, weren't you?"

I admitted that I was.

"Perhaps we should meet again to re-establish our relationship," she told me.

"Meet me at exactly noon on Thursday at the eucalyptus dell in Balboa Park, just off Sixth and Upas."

And with that, she hung up.

Thursday? It was then Sunday. How could I bear to wait four more days?

I knew the location she had mentioned quite well. It is where the San Diego Tai Chi group meets on Saturday mornings. I wondered how she knew that location. I would never dare ask her.

When Thursday at long last arrived, I was at the dell at eleven o'clock. I still hoped she approved of her devotees being anal.

I lay on the grass in the shade of one of the eucalyptus trees. A few people traversed the site as I lounged there. But, in the main, I had the area all to myself.

At noon, I grew apprehensive. No goddess yet.

The minutes crawled by, as they had for me back at the Ixtapa Ruiz. That son of a bitch Blake had certainly never shown himself to favor punctuality back then. But he did, eventually, appear in the bar.

My Circe had not popped into view at the prick of noon. Was I being stood up? Or would she, like her erstwhile slave, Blake, enjoy the torment she must know I would feel as I was kept waiting.

At precisely twelve thirty-one a vision emerged from a coppice.

It was not Circe. Nay, not she. For the Roman poet Ovid had referred to Circe as "the fire-red tressèd witch adorned in crimson robes."

The apparition that appeared resplendent in that enchanted dell was golden haired and clad in shining black leather.

It was my Venus in Leather.

But I had been warned not to so address her until she granted me permission to do so.

I sprang to my feet and rushed to the spot from which she reigned and threw myself at her feet.

"Goddess," I greeted as I kissed her booted foot. "You have returned."

She pulled her foot back, lifted it, and placed it firmly upon my neck. The discomfort was intense.

"Swine!" she exclaimed. "Speak only when permission to do so is granted."

Swine! Yes, we were certainly back to Circe/Swine mode.

With my head pressed mercilessly into the grass by the stiletto-heeled boot of the dominatrix-costumed elegant woman, I imagined what the scene must look like to anyone who happened to be strolling idly into the dell.

It was, I knew, a scene worthy of a modern artist of the caliber of a heroic painter like Jacques Louis David. The scene was set in an enchanted Arcadian grove. A regal, beautifully visaged dominatrix, with a cruel smile gracing her lips, stood there with her love-slave's neck pressed into the grassy swath…

Oh, what a scene! And I was such a dramatic part of it.

Heaven could offer no more lyric vision than this.

"Beg me to release you from the tyranny of my boot, in order that you might tell Circe your vile desires," my goddess said.

It was very definite, then, that it was safe for me to address her as Circe.

"O Circe," I managed to say, despite the difficulty of speaking while her boot was crushing my windpipe.

"I beg permission to address you."

She removed that painfully engaged boot and stepped back so I could sit up.

I quickly assumed a subservient position on my knees and gazed up into her gorgeous emerald-green eyes.

"Well, Pig," she said. "Out with it. What is on your mind?"

"It is you, Circe, who is on my mind," I responded.

"I know I may not yet refer to you as my ideal – my Venus in Leather. And yet, I plead that you might allow me the opportunity to prove myself worthy of so addressing you."

"And do you really expect me to embody this mythical ideal of yours?" she smirked. "What a romantic fool you are."

I assured her that despite her objections, I had truly sought her all my life. And that I was there to implore her to allow me to be her slave in order that I might convince her of my devotion.

"Were you to subject yourself to me," she warned. "You would be as great a fool as those who yielded themselves to Madame Pompadour or Catherine the Second. A selfish devil inhabited those dominating women, you know."

"No one ever mistook a goddess for a saint," I replied. "I warrant that you may be a devil in your own mind. You are a goddess in mine."

"Are you telling me then, that you are aware you are actually pleading to become my toy? That you would be willing to be mine to play with, to dandle, toss about and finally throw away or destroy at will?"

"Yes, Circe," I told her. "I agree to all that without reservation."

"Then," she smiled her cruel smile, "we will have to create a Purgatory where you can perhaps live out this mad obsession of yours. A Purgatory with a gate to Paradise, of course.

"Be aware that I have subjected other fools. And in other purgatories. You must never, ever consider yourself unique."

I did not have a clue what my idol was talking about. But I agreed with her, whatever it was she was suggesting.

"If you are fool enough, I will allow you to rent our own private Purgatory, where I will rule over you unrestrictedly.

"There will be financial costs to you, of course. You will have to rent a space where I will have our dungeon created. And you will have to bear the cost of refurbishing it with elements conducive to severe chastisement. For the word chastisement you may substitute the word 'torture.'

"And, of course, you will bear the cost of getting the studio absolutely soundproofed. Your shrieks of pain and agony must not cause alarm in the neighborhood. Although I will have you gagged from time to time, usually you will not be gagged because I thoroughly enjoy the cries of pain I elicit from my victims.

"But, be aware that following the agonies of purgatory, the blessings of paradise may await you.

"If it is your will to undergo subjugation, pain and humiliation at my hands, meet me at Bassam's Coffee House at the corner of Fourth Avenue and Market Street in the Gaslamp Quarter at ten o'clock tomorrow morning.

"You may now kiss my boot and remain prostrated until I have left the dell," she told me.

I gratefully kissed her boot, flung myself flat on the ground and remained thus until I knew sufficient time had passed to allow her to exit the scene.

The next morning found me at ten o'clock on my fourth cup of espresso and my third bran muffin at Bassam's. I had been there for close to an hour in nervous anticipation of my meeting with Wanda.

It was approaching quarter to eleven before she glided in, drawing attention from all the men customers and a fair number of the women as well.

She wore a bright red very tailored silk blouse and a shining black leather knee-length skirt. Her boots were simple black Wellingtons. Her purse was an enormous leather pouch and her leather beret sat jauntily atop her blonde curls.

Knockout!

She sat herself at my table and simply said, "Chai."

I went to the counter and ordered a chai for her and another black espresso for myself.

When I returned to our table, Wanda received her drink and sipped it silently.

"What now, Circe?" I asked.

She scowled at me and did not answer.

When she had finished her tea and delicately wiped her lips, she looked me fiercely in the eye.

"Unless spoken to…" she enunciated loud enough for everyone in the room to hear.

I filled in the blanks in my own mind.

Do not speak unless spoken to or having received my prior permission.
I nodded that I understood.

"In public – Wanda," she said in as loud a voice as she had used before.

I felt the eyes of everyone in the room fixed on me.

What goes on with the nerdy gentleman and the outspoken exotic woman in leather?

I understood her message. When she and I were clearly in slave-mistress mode, I was to call her Circe for now. In an openly public situation, she was to be known as Wanda.

There was so much I needed to learn about the rules involved in the special loving relationship I had with this woman.

In a soft voice that I had to strain to hear she told me:

"Across the street, Varken, is an old structure called the Farley Building that has been converted into a series of artists' studios. It is there that we will establish your purgatory."

Varken? Perhaps a term of endearment in Surinamese Dutch?

We left the coffee shop and proceeded across the street to the Farley Building. We located the building manager who enthusiastically showed us several available studios.

Wanda evidenced displeasure at the rooms on the west side of the building. They all had windows facing onto either Market Street or Fourth Avenue.

The studios aligned along the east wall were uniformly dark and windowless. I detected a sparkle of interest in my goddess' eyes when we were shown a pair of studios with a connecting door in the darkest, drabbest corner of the third floor.

She nodded at me. I got the picture.

And it was thus that I leased my own personal purgatory and Wanda's paradise in that building that housed artists.

Well, that is to say, it harbored traditional artists. With my Venus in Leather engaged in her exotic specialty, a true *artiste* was about to be added to the crew.

From the studios I had just rented, Wanda led me to a boutique called The Fetish Factory over on Sixth Avenue.

And in that store my idol went on a shopping spree such as I had never before witnessed.

The clerk on duty clearly spied immediately what kind of customers he had in his store. There was no doubt that Wanda and I were a domina and her new submissive. A female top and a male bottom. And that the lady would be purchasing instruments of torture to administer to the gentleman with the wallet who would pay for objects meant to inflict pain to his very own being.

As Wanda chose items with the eye of a connoisseur, I dutifully carried them over to the register counter.

Frankly, I did not know what many of the objects even were.

The following objects are just a few representatives of Wanda's purchases:

Whips, paddles, canes, riding crops, scourges, ropes, chains, collars, leashes, tethers, handcuffs, foot cuffs, a spanking bench, a bondage table, spreader bars, gags, masks, blindfolds, alligator clips, chained nipple clips, a dildo strap, dildos, ass plugs, anal beads, ball crushers...

Wanda told me to go over to the counter, pay for the purchases, and have them delivered, in my name, to the manager's office of the Farley Building at Fourth and Market.

"While you are paying the bill and making the arrangements, I will leave you," she told me.

"Tomorrow morning, at ten o'clock sharp, meet me again at Bassam's. And have a reputable building contractor with you who will work with me to convert our rentals into a Purgatory and a Paradise that will serve our purple needs."

I did not know what "purple needs" were exactly. But the sound gave me a case of delightful nervous shudders.

The next morning at ten, Todd McCreary, a contractor whose work I knew, met me at Bassam's.

And, contrary to her previous practices, Wanda came gliding into the coffee house at precisely ten as well.

So. She could be prompt when she decided to be.

I introduced Wanda to Todd and the three of us sat down to our drinks.

Wanda had a large folder with plans for the work she wanted done at the purgatory. Todd, to give him credit, did not bat an eye at the peculiar makeovers she wanted wrought. It was clear that he was to convert the studios into a torture chamber called Purgatory and an adjacent Purple

Chamber to be called Paradise. And I was sure he had no question as to who would be the torturer and who would be the victim on the purgatory side.

Or, about who would be the goddess and who the slave.

We went across the street, looked at the studios in their woeful emptiness and Todd told Wanda he would send me an estimate for the work my Venus had outlined.

It took Todd a full month to complete the project.

I can tell you the job was very expensive. The sound-proofing alone cost enough to cause me to borrow more money than was in the original estimate.

But, at the end of the month, both Purgatory and Paradise were completed.

Wanda and I met Todd there for the final inspection.

The studios had been marvelously converted from a couple of drab rooms to a splendiferously hideous torture chamber and a luxurious purple boudoir.

Wanda was delighted and I was ecstatic. Dominating the east wall of Purgatory were two massive crosses – one a Roman cross, the other an X-cross. They were each fitted with eyebolts and hooks at strategic spots for attaching a body (mine) securely into a position to endure creative flogging.

The spanking bench and bondage table stood on the south side of the room ready for securing a body (mine) in place for cruel whippings, paddlings, or other delightful unpleasantries.

Wanda's eyes gleamed when she spied the many pulleys attached to the ceiling, with ropes and chairs running through them and hooks, trapeze bars and other objects dangling from them.

The door leading to the other studio, Paradise, was located on the north wall. On each side of that door there were built-in shelves, bins, cabinets and hooks for the whips, cuffs, ropes, chains and other instruments and supplies which I had purchased at the Fetish Factory.

I believe it was the most perfectly fitted-out torture chamber in San Diego. And, an incomparable twin purple chamber. A site of great pride both to Venus and to her slave.

Wanda opened the door to the north chamber.

The three of us entered the Purple Chamber, Paradise, to admire the glamorously outfitted room with its oriental rug, four-poster bed, and armoires.

An elaborate crystal candelabra hung from the ceiling and there were candle sconces on all the walls.

Wanda herself had chosen every object in Paradise. It was, to my mind, a room befitting a goddess. The bitch goddess I had been seeking all my life.

Wanda told Todd and me to shout and scream as loud as we could when she stepped out into the hallway to test the soundproofing Todd had done.

When she stepped out and closed the door, Todd and I made a truly raucous racket. There was no way that my screams under Venus' whip would ever exceed our combined sound in volume.

When Wanda re-entered the room, her pleasure was evident.

I handed Todd the check for his work and supplies. He handed me a receipt, and Purgatory was ready to provide the chastisement and humiliation only a perfectly appointed torture chamber can offer. And the Purple Chamber, Paradise, awaited the goddess' pleasure.

Wanda told me to meet her in Purgatory the next night on the prick of midnight.

To tell the truth, it was not so much that she *told* me. What she did was *order* me to be there.

She and I both understood that I preferred to be *ordered* than told. *Who wouldn't?*

I arrived at Fourth and Market at eleven forty-five. It was a dark night with no moon in the sky. The Gaslamp Quarter is usually quite lively at the witching hour, and there was revelry aplenty at the bistros and clubs over on Fifth Avenue. But a somber quiet hovered over the corner where I stood gazing at the building which housed my purgatory.

As I entered the building I trembled with erotic trepidation. The squeaky sounds my shoes pressed onto the stair steps seemed to me to bode promises of deadly delight.

At the prick of midnight, I inserted my key into the lock of the door to Purgatory.

I quickly stepped in and closed the door behind me. There was a lone candle burning in the room, casting a flickering light over the scene.

I of course knew what was expected of me. I removed all my clothing, placed it neatly in the southwest corner of the room, hastened to the center of the chamber and faced the northern wall toward the gate that led to Paradise. I then dropped to my knees to await the entrance of my goddess.

When I heard to gate to Paradise open, I dared daze upward to behold my goddess illuminated by the flickering light of the single candle.

She was attired in the black leather cat suit I had last seen her wearing in Ixtapa. She had been stunning there. She was resplendent now.

She held a riding crop in one hand and a cat-o'-nine-tails in the other. Her pose was regal. The expression on her gorgeous face reflected both scorn and contempt.

My heartbeat quickened with love and adoration.

The sight of the scourges she held in her hands demonstrated undeniably how much she adored me. The cat-o'-nine-tails was a loving remembrance of my beating in Ixtapa. And the riding crop showed she remembered how I had loved the whippings Aunt Sarah had given me in Claremont.

Yes. No doubt about it. Wanda loved me.

She approached me with her stately swagger, the knotted ends of the scourges she held in her hands trailing her path. At the sight of her approach I feared I would swoon.

When she stood in front of me, I lowered my body to the floor and kissed her left boot.

While still bent in groveling position before her, I had to ask about our current identities in this new and wonderful venue.

I knew she would punish me for speaking without having received prior permission. And since I longed for flagellation anyway, I quickly spilled out my question.

"O Divine Goddess," I implored. "Tell me, how I may address you now that I encounter you in this purgatory of your exquisite design. I cannot believe that you now appear to me in the avatar of Circe."

Zing! Zing! Zing!

The delicious sting from the business end of the riding crop assailed my exposed naked back with instant ferocity.

"You would be well advised," Wanda's inexorable voice hissed. "To speak only with my prior permission.

"With the provision you have of this worthy den of castigation, I am pleased to reward you with the privilege of recognizing me as Venus."

"My Venus in Leather," I could not restrain myself from proclaiming.

Zing! Zing! Zing! Zing! Zing! Zing!

Oh, glorious!

"Yes," she continued when she had vented her fury at my pretentious outburst.

"Now that I am revealed to you in this purple veiled location," she announced, "you shall henceforth respond to the name *Anchises*."

I was well acquainted with the name. And I immediately recognized its relevance to my relationship with my Venus.

For Anchises, in the classical tradition, was the mortal who fell in love with Venus, and to whom the goddess returned affection.

But the manner in which she reciprocated his ardor was with divine punishment.

Thus, if Wanda was the goddess Venus, I would be Anchises, her lover, who welcomed her discipline as proof of her love.

"Now, Anchises," Venus addressed me. "Tell me the purpose of your visit here tonight."

"To worship you and to bear pain and humiliation at your hands," I answered her truthfully.

"Just so," she agreed. "And I will gladly administer both.

"But, I know you are aware that I am merciless in my inflictions. Thus, in practicality, in the world of sadism and masochism, there is *always* the need for the submissive to have a "safe word" available to him.

"Whenever the punishment approaches a level of true physical danger, the 'bottom' needs a word which will halt the procedure and will initiate immediate aid to his mortal distress.

"Do you understand the concept of the safe word?"

"Yes, Goddess," I assured her. "I understand that henceforth, in a true physical emergency, I may invoke the safe word and the relationship of goddess to devotee will cease and all castigation on your part will stop. Until such invocation, I may plead with you to halt punishment without avail.

"With that understanding, Goddess, inform me. What is to be the word?"

"Rhadamanthus!" she told me.

From my reading I knew all about Rhadamanthus and the myths surrounding him. He was one of the judges who dwelt in the Greek and Roman Underworld.

"The name of the god who can grant a damned soul release from Purgatory!" I exclaimed.

"I just knew you would understand," Venus scoffed.

"You are *such* a dork."

And a cute *dork, too,* I smiled.

I was happily aware that a new relationship between my dominatrix and myself had just congealed. I kissed her boot again in token of my acceptance.

"Arise, Anchises," Venus commanded. "And proceed to the spanking bench where you will be able to relish again the pleasures you last received in Claremont."

I had no doubt whatsoever about which piece of furniture in Purgatory was the spanking bench.

It looked not unlike a *prie-dieu*. You know, those French kneeling benches with a shelf above to hold a prayer-book? In the case of the spanking bench, though, the shelf is designed to hold the sub's naked abdomen as he leans over it. His hands are shackled to the rings near the floor and his feet fit into widely spaced slots on the spanking side.

As Venus bound me across the piece of furniture, I exulted in the feeling of how gloriously my bare ass was exposed for a jolly good beating.

Venus played the riding crop upon my butt with an expertise that seemed to exceed Aunt Sarah's. But then, in all fairness, there was not a spanking bench in my aunt's home. So it is hardly fair to make odious comparisons.

And whereas Aunt Sarah seldom lashed me more than twenty strokes during a session, Venus had hardly even warmed up at twenty. I counted out the strokes aloud at her bidding, through my cries of agony. And on this first occasion on the spanking bench, I grew breathless at the fifty-second slash as the pain morphed into ecstasy.

During the entire flagellation, Venus verbally excoriated me with terms like "queer" (which she used in the Victorian sense of deviant rather than homosexual), "rabble", "dreg", "raff", and "sordes". All the insulting terms were drawn from her reading of Victorian novelists like Trollope, Thackeray and Titmarsh.

And I acknowledged in my heart that the insults she flung at me really did fit who and what I am. Because I really am a crummy little shit, you know.

Because of the state of heightened awareness that her thrashing elicited from me, I yearned for even deeper pain. But I dared not tell her so. For my goddess denied me speech.

I was permitted only the wails of anguish or…the gods forbid…my safe word, Rhadamanthus.

Moreover, I felt quite sure that more intense pain awaited me as the night would progress, anyway.

Practically reading my mind, my Venus in Leather released me from the bench and ordered me to stand spread-eagle at the X-cross that was affixed to the east wall.

As I faced the wall, Venus pinioned my wrists to the upper extensions and my ankles to the lower ones. She adjusted the X to spread me well beyond my comfort zone. More divine discomfort.

With me in my extremely vulnerable position, Venus was free to truly demonstrate her expertise with the cat-o'-nine-tails. Uttering a constant rant of abuse about my grievous deficiencies, she lashed my back, shoulders and thighs with a savage ferocity that would have been hailed enthusiastically by British sea captains like the sadistic Captain Bligh of the HMS Bounty.

I shrieked. I moaned. I cried. I wailed. I even found myself pleading for her to desist, saying I could bear no more.

But the word Rhadamanthus did not escape my lips.

And after three dozen flagellations I swooned from pain, exhaustion and rapture.

When she released me from the cross, I slunk to the floor like a dropped marionette. Venus retrieved her riding crop from where she had left it at the spanking bench and stood over my prostrate form.

She began to beat me with the crop blow after vicious blow.

"Get up on your hands and knees, Asshole," she growled. "Stop lying there like a dog turd, you hunk of shit. I need you to crawl through yonder door to join me in Paradise."

With my last ounce of strength I managed to haul my grievously bruised and bleeding body out of its prone position so I could crawl on my hands and knees behind her as she marched triumphantly through the north door into Paradise.

As I went on all fours towards the door I realized that on this first night of my life as her slave, Venus had actually treated me lightly. There was no doubt in my mind that I had tasted only a tiny drop of the pain of Purgatory. I looked forward to much more pain in my future chastisements in that hideously delightful room.

When I managed to drag my ass into the purple room with its oriental rugs, chandelier and four-poster bed, Venus demanded that I gaze up upon her face so she could address me as I adored her.

"In most instances," she informed me. "When you bear your well-deserved punishment in a fashion that pleases me, we will end the session here in Paradise where you will enjoy dessert.

"Would you care to enjoy a bit of dessert, Anchises?"

"Nothing would delight me more," I enthused, reviving from the stupor I had been reduced to.

"In that case, you must prepare me for your delectation," she told me. "Arise, worshipfully remove all clothing from my body and place it fastidiously in the armoire over there in the northeast corner.

"When you finish that task, crawl over to the bed where I will await your coming."

I knew that "coming" would not involve any ejaculations on my part. That type of coming would have to wait until I got home.

When I had undressed her and taken care of her leather clothing, I crawled, as ordered, to the magnificent antique bed. She was reclining there like a classical odalisque.

As I crawled up onto the bed at her feet she looked at me with what I interpreted as a loving smile.

"This evening your reward for good behavior is access to my feet," she announced in dulcet tones.

Feet! My foot fetish is in close proximity to my leather fetish.

If allowing me to engage in my foot fetish did not prove her deep love for me, I do not know the meaning of "love."

"You are to take my feet in hand," she instructed me. "One at a time."

Oh, those beautiful, dainty, lovely feet. My scrotum gave my balls a clasping squeeze.

"You are to suck each toe, individually, lasciviously. Once having fellated each toe with intense devotion, you may run your tongue between the toes with the ardor with which a gifted cunnilingist gives head to a fragrant cunt.

"When you have performed these functions to your heart's content, you are to lick the entire surface of each foot, giving gifted tongue to the arches in particular.

"But, always keep in mind, Anchises, that while doing the kissing, licking and tongue probing, I expect your hands to ceaselessly massage the foot you are giving head to with tender devotion."

Oh, joy! Oh, bliss! Exercising my passion on the divine feet of my goddess was the most elegant dessert I had ever been offered.

My delight was enhanced by Venus' dictum that while in Purgatory or Paradise I must not, in any way or fashion, pleasure my own dick. The pain that was inflicted on me by the extreme horniness of my punishments and my subsequent reward was nearly too much painful ecstasy to bear.

The most exquisite pain of all.

Venus specifically forbade me to jack off until I got back home and had snuggled down into my bed.

When I had satisfied my foot fetish to the utmost, I gave each of Venus' feet a prolonged kiss and exited paradise in my subservient crawl.

Back in Purgatory I got dressed and left the building.

I have no idea how long Venus lingered in the paradisiacal bed after I had left.

At home and naked in my own bed, I gloried in how my Venus in Leather had enraptured me.

I loved her. I adored her. My supreme happiness was in being her slave.

And in memory of my stay in Purgatory, and then in Paradise, I jerked off into a truly blessed ejaculation.

CHAPTER FOUR

URBANE SLAVERY

I will not elaborate on the six months of sessions my Venus and I passed in our encounters behind the purple veil.

I will simply sum up by revealing to you the last session we had at our Purgatory-Paradise.

Venus had summoned me to meet her in Purgatory at the stroke of midnight.

I crawled into the room, disrobed, and waited in breathless anticipation for her entry from Paradise as I groveled on the floor facing the north wall.

When the door from Paradise opened, I looked up and saw that my Venus in Leather was holding her rattan cane in hand. She was followed into Purgatory by another woman.

The newcomer to our frolic was enormous, nude, gorgeous, voluptuous, and black.

Venus halted before she got to where I was crouched so her companion could step around her and lay her stunning body down horizontally some two feet in front of me.

"Anchises," Venus told me. "Tonight we will dispense with the ritual of you kissing of my boot as a symbol of your abasement. Instead, you may demonstrate your devotion to me by running your tongue over every inch of Rachel's body."

Hmm. Rachel? Delighted to meet you, I'm sure.

Rachel was a true tongue-treat. My tongue did not miss as much as a square centimeter of that luscious brown skin of hers. (To be more precise, not even a cubic centimeter.)

I laved her nipples, cunt and clit to perfection, of course. Her asshole, mouth, armpits and nostrils got well worked over. Her feet, toes, hands and fingers got sucked and fucked by my tongue and mouth.

One might think that was devotion enough to pay to the female body Venus bade me tongue-and-mouth swab. But how wrong one would be.

For, while I was ministering to that chocolate hued epidermis, Venus was beating every exposed surface of my own skin with her vicious rattan cane.

Rachel was moaning in bliss. I was slobbering and humming with exaltation. I was also moaning and sobbing with pain from the beating I was receiving. And Venus was cursing and scolding me with divine fury.

I was in hopes these devotions of mine to Venus would continue world without end. Amen.

But, alas! After all is said and done, there remains but one law in our universe. A law which prevails even over the "Laws of the Medes and the Persians, which altereth not."

It is decreed that everything that exists must come to an end.

When I was done with her, Rachel passed out from pure pleasure. I, myself, collapsed with painfully burning vivid crimson welts covering my entire body. And Venus' lovely cane-wielding arm got plumb worn out.

I collapsed on the floor in a stupor. When I regained consciousness, Rachel was gone and Venus was sitting in a chair gazing contemptuously at my bruised body.

All that had occurred thus far was merely a prelude to the main act which, I knew, would soon follow.

Venus arose from her chair, assumed her stately pose, and excoriated me.

"Anchises, you fucking sluggard," she hissed. "Are you planning to lollygag there on the floor in a morass of self pity all night long? Get your sorry ass turned around and crawl over to the bondage table this minute."

Oh, Boy! The bondage table. What delights awaited me there this time?

I hoisted my anticipatory body up onto the table and lay down on my back. Venus strapped my torso and head down snuggly, leaving my legs free of restraint.

The next thing I knew, she had slapped separate ringed cuffs around each of my ankles. I wondered what *that* was all about.

I was facing the ceiling, of course, taking in all those fascinating pulleys with various attachments to their ropes that dangled overhead.

Oh, look! Two of those ropes up there, the ones with the hooks. They were being lowered.

It looks like my legs will be taking a ride!

Sure enough, Venus attached one of the hooks to the ring on my left foot and one onto my right.

She told me to lift my legs up as high and as wide apart as I could manage.

With a series of yanks on her end of the ropes, Venus had my legs pulled up towards that ceiling and spread out into a wide V. My ass was raised off the table about three feet while my head and torso were strapped down tight against the bondage bench. My stiff prick was quivering with delight. It clearly enjoyed the novelty of the situation.

"Now, listen, Stupid," Venus was saying. "I have a nice ice bucket here next to your bondage table. And guess what is in it."

"Ice cubes?" I asked.

With her bare palm she whacked my suspended butt with as sound a smack as I'd ever felt.

"Wrong, Asshole," she chided.

"What I have here are ice dildos."

Now fancy that! Who would have thought?

She freed my right hand from its restraint and lubricated it well with Astrolube. I could not imagine what kind of treat she had in store for me.

"Now, you depraved dipshit," she said. "I plan to chastise you tonight with a trial by fire and ice.

Fire? Over the past six months Venus had burned off my pubic hair with the lit end of a cigar. She had splattered me with hot candle wax. And she had touched heated needles to the most sensitive areas of my skin. What more could she possibly do with fire?

Ice? What a novelty. She had never punished me with ice before.

I figured that was where the ice dildos would come in. But, for the life of me, I couldn't imagine how she would use them.

"And," I asked myself. "Why she was she freeing my right hand?" But I knew better than to conjecture about that.

"The procedure you will participate in involves something you love to do," she told me. "As a matter of fact, it is undoubtedly your very favorite private activity."

I knew what my favorite private activity was. But I wondered whether Venus would know.

"When you are all alone in bed at night, what activity delights you the most?" she asked.

"Whacking off," I admitted.

"Bravo," Venus replied.

Obviously she was not at all surprised.

"I never doubted that was what you loved to do from the moment a little jerk-off like you entered my life."

I love compliments. My Venus in Leather was an adept at flattery.

"I have forbidden you to so much as touch your teenie weenie in my presence heretofore," she reminded me. "But tonight, you will masturbate up a storm while enjoying the pain of fire and ice."

I do, indeed, love to jack off. So I thought my goddess had come up with a capital idea. Fire and ice be damned.

My right hand tingled in anticipation of entertaining my peter.

My Venus reached into the ice bucket and pulled out one of those cocksicles she had mentioned.

She held it before my eyes so I could take a good gander at it.

Wow! It was impressive. If it was molded from some actual man, he had to have been the best hung dude in the country.

While I admired the dildo's magnificent dimensions, Venus asked me to guess what she was going to do with it.

It seemed to me there were two prime possibilities. She would either have me suck it, or...

Oh, no! Not up my ass!

I hoped against hope that I could steer her thinking into the option that involved my oral cavity.

"You are going to make me suck that cocksickle." I ventured optimistically.

"Wrong! You fucking pervert," she leered. "No lovely icy cocksucking for you, my dear."

She called me "my dear." See! She really does love me.

"You Americans have a quaint expression... Now what is it?," she asked. "Oh, yes. 'Cornhole.' I am going to cornhole you with this dildo you so quaintly call a cocksickle."

What a revolting idea that *was.*

"That will be the 'ice' part of your chastisement."

"And the fiery part?" I wondered aloud.

"You cannot even guess," she taunted.

She pressed the bulbous tip of the cocksickle into my ass cleft. *Brr!*

She pushed it until it made arctic contact with my asshole. *Yikes! Double brr!*

"You are going to freeze my ass off, Goddess," I joked.

Venus was not amused. She gave me a sharp slap to my balls as a reprimand.

Now THAT hurt. No more dumb jokes.

As she kept the bulb pressed against my anus, Venus informed me, "Now you can begin to play with that pathetic dick of yours, Fruitcake."

Despite the intense pain in my balls and the uncomfortable chilling sensation in my ass, I was able to administer loving attention to my dick.

As she pressed the cocksickle past my sphincters and up into my colon, the pain in my balls diminished appreciably.

As I pumped away on my engorged dong, Venus ran the icy dildo up and down my shit-pipe, giving me a cornholing that defies description.

As that freezing hardon grazed my prostate gland, a sharp pain coursed up from my balls to my piss-hole.

Although I continued pumping with my hand, the intense pain that had suddenly turned my cock-knob from crimson to purple caused my entire body to spasm.

There was no way that my masturbation could lead to an ejaculation while my prostate was freezing. If there was a Hell, I figured I was in it.

It seemed forever before the goddam cocksickle melted. But the heat engendered in my body finally did the trick.

Man, O man. What a nifty treat for a masochist *that* had been.

Could anything more fiendish follow? Unimaginable.

As I began to relax, I realized that I had not even heard the reproaches Venus had been heaping on me as she maneuvered that weird dildo up and down my ass canal.

"Did you enjoy your freezing cornhole, Anchises?" she asked.

"Delightfully uncomfortable, Venus," I told her. "Thank you very much."

I continued diddling my cock as I carried on that merry little conversation with my idol.

She picked up a long, curved ivory butt-plug from the taboret. She had used it on me many times before in most painfully delightful ways. I was sure she had a novel new quirk to add to its wickedness.

The arch of the plug was such as to cause the tip to press against my freezing prostate with a decided pressure when the bottom handle was held correctly.

Ooo! Heavenly!

Venus held a little bottle in her left hand as she held the plug in her right.

A distinctive bottle. I was familiar with it. Where had I seen it before? In restaurants! Yes. It was a condiment.

Oh, no! I suddenly realized what it was. Tabasco sauce.

Venus was liberally dousing the plug with Tabasco Sauce. Hot sauce up my ass?!

I was not sure I could take it. What was my safe word? Something or someone to do with the Underworld. Oh, yes. Rhadamanthus.

I had better have the word in my consciousness if the next caper proved too much for me.

All this cogitating went on while I gladsomely continued to flog the bishop.

In a waggish mood, Venus splattered a couple of drops of the hot sauce onto my balls. Although the effect was not as physically irritating as she probably hoped, it was certainly damned uncomfortable.

But I ceased paying attention to it immediately when she placed the Tabasco covered tip of the plug directly on the pink bud of my shithole.

I screamed bloody murder. I could not control myself.

I caught the gleam of joy in my goddess' eyes. The lovelight fairly sparkled.

If the mere touch of that wicked dildo could be that excruciating, what would I be experiencing when she rammed that sucker up into my ass!

I could hardly wait.

I did not even think, at the time, to joke about what a "hot ass" I was. The playful part of my brain had quite shut down.

Venus ran that hot rod up and down my ass, giving me a cornholing that made me shriek so loud I wondered if the room's soundproofing was sufficient to screen out my bellows. I certainly did not want to alert the police to come crashing into the room to find me trussed up, jacking off, and being ass-fucked by a leather-clad Surinamese beauty wielding a Tabasco-coated butt plug.

Thankfully Todd McCreary had done a very creditable job of isolating sound within the confines of Purgatory.

Up and down my anal tract went the dildo. Up and down my love shaft went my right hand. My gasps and moans spurted from my convulsive lungs.

The result of the sensations up my ass and in contact with my prostate and the "self abuse" I was so heartily engaged in, caused me to shoot an enormous, excruciatingly painful wad right out of my pecker and onto my gaping face.

I could swear that I unloaded my balls completely of the hottest jism that ever besmirched a jerkoff's features.

I was totally spent from my ordeal. My poor whang throbbed with pain. And I was exhausted from my suspended toes to my flushed face.

The whole experience had been a real gas.

And, to add to my pleasure, I observed that Venus was in a heightened state of euphoria.

How that woman loved to pleasure me.

From her bountiful kindness, Venus allowed me close to a quarter hour to recuperate from the harrowing experience of fire and ice.

When I was able to breathe normally again, she lowered the pulley ropes, unhooked my footcuffs, unbound my left hand and let me drop my limp body down off the table and onto the floor with a dull thud.

After a few painful stretches, I was able to sit up fairly straight and look around.

My eyes took in the familiar sights of Purgatory and at length landed on the gorgeous shape of my leather-clad goddess who was tapping the tip of a boot on the floor while waiting for me to get myself onto my hands and knees to join her at the X-cross over on the east wall.

As I crawled over to her, I made out that my Venus held a riding crop in one hand and a cat-o'-nine-tails in the other.

Oh, goodie. Two different kinds of lashings awaited me

"Get yourself up there on that cross, facing me, holding onto the upper grips. And spread your legs to the full extent of the lower bars," she ordered.

This was a rare treat indeed. Instead of being affixed to the cross, I would get to hold myself there without the benefit of manacles.

By the time I had arranged my body on the cross in position for whatever form of torture Venus had in store for me, she had set aside the cat and was snapping the crop in the air.

A flicked riding crop produces such a genteel sound. It breathes of equitational jaunts in the countryside with one's horsey friends.

Venus took careful measure of the distance between the two of us. Her practice flips of the thong finally satisfied her. She was in position to assure that the knotted end would inflict the maximum stinging sensation as it unfurled onto whichever of my bodily parts she intended to strike.

She pulled her right arm back, raised it up above her head, and gave her wrist a flip that propelled the lash directly at me.

I blinked, flinched and yelled. I could not restrain my automatic reactions.

In that split second I could not anticipate where the damned knot would land.

Jesus!

Right on my left nipple.

What precision that woman had. What a painful target she had chosen. It hurt like bloody Hell.

I nearly lost my grip on the handles from which I was hanging.

The look of glee on Venus' face showed the pleasure she took in the accuracy of her scourging and at the violence of my reaction.

She continued flicking the whip so that the strand hit first one nipple, then another. Not in a predictable sequence. I could never tell which of my rosebud male-tits would get the next blow. I knew that by the third flip I was bleeding quite copiously from each dug. And that as the pain grew close to unbearable the smile on my goddess's face gleamed ever brighter.

I lost count of the number of strikes I sustained. In her kindness, Venus did not require me to count out the blows aloud.

Eventually, (was it around the twentieth severe blow?), I lost my grip on the handles and slumped down onto the floor in a dizzy swoon.

I had reached the breakthrough from pain to ecstasy about halfway through the exercise. I was in Nirvana.

As I lay on the floor, Venus applied medicated salve to my bloody chest and she affixed bandages.

She was my own little Florence Nightingale.

When I was capable of squirming into an upright sitting position, Venus told me she still had a final chastisement for me.

I showed her my enthusiasm for whatever it might be with a nod of my head.

"Anchises, Dear," she said. "I have decided to leave San Diego. I will tell you all about it during dessert.

"I know you would be disappointed if I did not regale you with a final scourging on your back with the cat-o'-nine-tails before I leave.

"So *do* get yourself up off the floor there so I can get these manacles onto your wrists and ankles. I have to affix you to the cross nice and tight so your back will form a lovely target for the cat."

I had regained enough control to be able to struggle up onto my feet. Venus clamped the cuffs on me and I shuffled up to the cross, extended myself spread-eagle, and immediately found myself bound for punishment.

The following punishment, which was the last I ever received in that Purgatory I had paid for, was the final flourish of our San Diego sado-masochistic rites.

It consisted of four dozen whooshes of the cat laid across my back with an intensity worthy of one descended from Olympus.

Four dozen strokes was the maximum number that wondrous creature ever inflicted on me during our San Diego romance. And that is what I received on that occasion.

The session I had endured that night had inflicted more pain on my receptive body than I had ever before experienced.

The beating I had received with the rattan cane while I sucked and licked every inch of Rachel's luscious body had been a pleasantly tingling warm-up. The fire and ice torture which followed offered new pain sensations that I would never have dreamed possible before. The consequent flaying of my nipples reduced me to a rumpled heap of bliss.

And the traditional four dozen kisses of the wicked cat upon my abused back rounded out a near perfect evening.

All that remained to make it eternally memorable was dessert.

As I mentioned, that final session I had experienced in my San Diego Purgatory had inflicted more pain to my body than I had ever previously born. And it had rewarded me with the most pleasure as well. As in the expression "no pain, no gain."

For what I had achieved during the torture session was an actual transcendence.

Pain releases endorphins in the brain which stimulate a feeling of euphoria better than alcohol, cocaine, marijuana or opium can produce. I know. I have tried all those. And they are synthetic. Pain, on the other hand, is real. Excruciatingly real.

Athletes like boxers and marathon runners know what we masochists are talking about when we say we get high on pain. The pain they experience, runners call it "hitting the wall," is as addictive as any drug. And for many muscle-men, pumping iron is as addictive .

And, when the suffering is carried to extremes, it can lead to a similar other-worldly ecstatic euphoria.

When you are high on your own endorphins, you can never go back to drugs or alcohol again to get that wonderful transcendence.

From my earliest spankings, I had formed a basis on which to gauge all fake external joy-makers. Instead of drugs or alcohol, I would choose good old masochistic pain any time.

As I have mentioned, Mommy Dearest and "Auntie" Gertrude beat me regularly, teaching me to experience the "endorphin high" that comes from sustained pain.

When I grew up, I paid whores to beat me to the point of experiencing true ecstasy.

Then, when I went off to college, my Aunt Sarah kindly beat the hell out of me to the point of exaltation.

In Mexico, I got beatings on the cheap from the whores.

But right there, in San Diego, in my own purchased Purgatory, my Venus favored me with the greatest exhilaration I thought I could ever achieve.

Ruminating on these thoughts, I crawled my prostrate form that lay at the foot of that X-cross, foot by foot, yard by yard towards the door that opened to Paradise. I knew that in that room, I would receive a dessert, bread of the angels, from my goddess. And I would hear from her own lips about the change of venue she had alluded to when she had told me that she had decided to leave San Diego.

I wondered just where she and I would be going together.

When I had crawled into Paradise and closed the door behind me by backing up and bumping it with my bare ass, I searched the room for my Venus.

Oh, what joy! I spied her in her full naked radiant beauty reclining on the four-poster bed, her upper body propped up on an enormous pillow.

She was watching me with a stunning smile on her face.

Without uttering a word, she motioned for me to crawl over to the bed. I did so, and then slithered up onto the sheets. I curled up at her feet and awaited her next orders.

"You have born my scourges and humiliations bravely, Anchises," she complimented me. "I have been delighted and refreshed by your moans, tears and groveling during this, our last tryst in San Diego.

"And now you have arrived in Paradise where you will be rewarded with the divine dessert deserved by martyrs like yourself.

"As a special treat tonight, *panis angelicus* awaits you. For I am going to condescend to allow you to fondle, kiss and lick my derrière to your heart's content."

Delight of delights. It was more than I could have hoped for. More than *panis angelicus*. I was being offered *anus Veneris*. It was possible that neither Adonis nor Anchises had ever been granted such a boon. To fondle, kiss and lick those rosy cheeks and that pink asshole without a limit on time or enthusiasm was more than I had ever wished for or dreamed of.

Venus glided down from her elegant pillow, gracefully rolled herself over into a crouch, and exposed her lovely rump to me. Her ass-cheeks glowed in the light of the candelabra. I feared I might just faint away in adoration.

I commenced with massaging those twin moons, one hand on each orb. I squeezed, I pinched, I nipped, I rubbed, I tickled.

Venus' moans and purrs gladdened my heart and dong. With each of her utterances of loving contentment a fresh surge of blood coursed into my delighted prick.

After a lengthy period of manual and digital attention was paid to those delightful buns, it was time for my lips, tongue and teeth to administer pious devotion to them.

Her cheeks had morphed from alabaster white to pale rose as a consequence of the ministrations of my hands and fingers. Now, as I licked, kissed, nibbled and bit, the pinkish hue deepened to a decided crimson tone.

Oh, how my goddess soughed, sighed and whimpered in response to the loving nipping and bussing of her precious bottom.

All this caused me not only delight, but suffering as well. For, as nearly always in her presence, I was forbidden to give manual attention to my throbbing dick.

When Venus' ass-cheeks had received their well-deserved attention for a period of perhaps an hour, I was impelled to place a palm on each protuberance and spread those lovely mounds apart.

And there it was. Staring me in the eye. That puckered pink bud of her divine asshole.

I could gaze on that beauty for hours on end. But what would such devotion do for the goddess? Dessert involved not only the esthetic delight to my artistic soul but also the accompaniment of corporal pleasure for my deity.

So, after only a few minutes of devoted ogling of that bunghole, I burrowed my face into the crevice and slobbered madly all over the target.

I licked. I sucked. I ran my tongue up into the hole. I gurgled. I sighed. I fluttered my tongue.

My exuberance was accompanied by raucous laughter on the part of my divine partner.

At length, she collapsed face down onto the bed's surface in a paroxysm of chuckles that, for a while, made her appear quite mad.

I could not refrain from giving vent to my own merriment and matched Venus' insanity outburst by outburst.

Eventually, the goddess turned her body so she was facing the mirror on the ceiling. I lay next to her to revel in the sight of the two of us still rollicking in our convulsions.

Her tits jiggled merrily in accompaniment to her risibility. My erect peter was performing a jig in time to my laughter.

My left hand was trembling in its frustration at not being allowed to fondle the breast and nipple of my bedmate. And my right hand tingled at being proscribed from encircling my yearning phallus.

In due time, both Venus and I regained our sanity and our composure.

When we were both calm enough to lie languid, Venus bade me slip off the bed and sit on the floor facing up at her.

She was kind enough to sit on the edge of the bed, feet dangling toward the floor, knees wide-spread so that I was gazing fondly up at her fully exposed cunt.

I had a direct view of the very core of the Goddess of Love. My hardon was aimed at that most desirable bull's-eye.

"Well, now, Anchises," Venus asked. "What would you have me tell you?"

I informed her that I was intrigued with her indication that we were quitting our Purgatory-Paradise in San Diego.

"Yes," she told me. "The sado-masochistic relationship we have engaged in here is all very well. But it is beginning to disenchant me."

"Disenchant?" I questioned.

"Yes, My Dear. Disenchant," she repeated.

How I loved to hear her call me "her dear."

"For here in America, you can only play-act being my slave. And in San Diego I am far from being your lawful dominant mistress. I must be allowed to exercise actual, legal power over you or I cannot be satisfied.

Nor, I truly believe, can you achieve the state of satisfactory slavishness for which you yearn."

She explained to me that in her country she had always had slaves. That if we were to go there, my slavery would no longer be a part-time matter as it was in California. It would be actual slavery, twenty-four seven.

"Is slavery actually legal in your country?" I wondered aloud.

I did not realize that slavery still was legal in Surinam.

Venus laughed.

"Slavery is not legally legal in Surinam," she told me. "But it is practiced in remote areas of the rainforest. When the Netherlands emancipated our slaves in the nineteenth century, the institution ceased in the northern regions. But it was never abandoned in the South where both masters and slaves have always found the relationship mutually satisfactory."

I understood.

In America, the use of certain drugs like marijuana and cocaine is illegal. Yet, in many communities the ingestion of the substances is widespread. So people who are quite respectable, even eminent, feel free to ignore what they consider unfair laws. The same acceptance could just as well apply to slavery in foreign lands.

After all. The State of Mississippi did not ratify the Fourteenth Amendment to the Constitution that abolished slavery until 1995. In a sense, slavery was still legal according to Mississippi law nearly until the Twenty First Century!

I told her I understood that there had to still be places in the world where slavery existed by mutual consent of both owners and slaves.

"I now know that you were born and raised in such an area," I told her. "Therefore, being mistress of others who belong to you feels quite natural.

"Here in North America you have found men who need to be subjugated by a woman who, like you, is comfortable dominating them. And, as you have discovered, I am one of those men.

"I truly love you so much that I want to be your absolute slave. I want to be in a land where there is nothing whatsoever that can interfere with your will, with your cruelty, and with your very special kind of love for me. I want to live where I would be subject to your slightest whim, where I would have to respond to your slightest beck and call every moment of every day."

Venus turned more serious than I had ever seen her.

"Do you truly love me that much?" she asked.

"I do, Venus," I told her.

"Then I would like to own you body and soul, Anchises," she avowed. "I am bored with dominating play-acting slaves like you and Blake and Rich and Frank…

"I told you outright that I need slaves, toys and playthings in abundance. You just might be the toy I take back with me when I finally return to my home in the rainforest.

"If you agree to accompany me there, you will no longer have any rights whatsoever. There will be no limit to my power over you. You will have no more worth than a dog or even an inanimate object like a stone or a turd.

"You will be mine. My plaything. You will be a thing I can break into pieces should I seek an hour's amusement. You will be nothing. And I, naturally, will be everything.

"I can assure you that under those conditions I will be much crueler to you than I have ever been heretofore."

I told her I certainly hoped so. And that I was ready to follow her to Surinam on the morrow on those conditions if she would have me.

"Not so fast, Anchises," she continued. "Before I allow you to take such a step, you will have to prove yourself.

"To begin with, let us see if you can function as my lickspittle servant, my cringing factotum, here in San Diego. I will set up some situations to see how base and groveling you can be here in these familiar settings.

"If that works out, I will allow you to attempt a more elaborate test of your ability to be subservient abroad."

Abroad! I loved the thought of going abroad with my goddess. But what location was she thinking of?

"We will go to Italy," she explained. "To Florence. I love that city. You will act the part of my subservient, fawning servant there.

"Then, if I find that you are able to please me with your subservience here in San Diego, and in Florence, I will allow you to sign a contract in which you relinquish all right to personal freedom. And you will grant me full power over your body, soul and physical existence. Then, we will depart for South America and the tropical rain forests of Surinam."

I gazed at this amazing woman with abject love and devotion.

"You are so cute, Leo," she gushed.

Leo! Not Anchises!

This was the mortal Wanda addressing the earthling Leo. This coming to earth literally caused my balls to tingle. The immortal woman still found the worthless Leo *cute!*

Wanda elaborated.

"Your devotion to me exceeds that of all the other men I have ever dominated. I know you would be absolutely smashing if I were to beat you to a pulp."

Smashing and *smashed, apparently.*

"I just might beat you to death sometime, you know," she smiled.

"You seek martyrdom so fiercely, don't you, you pitiful sap? And you must have guessed the truth about me. I am turned on by death.

"Oh, Leo," she said suddenly, in a new and passionate voice. "I want you to fuck me. Now!

"Come now, my martyr. Fuck me out of my mind.

"And then, after we have achieved an earthly ecstasy here in our trysting spot tonight, we will see how you deal with public humiliation on the morrow. I have some lovely trials to put you through.

"Fuck me," she said. So fuck her I did.

It was the pinnacle experience of my life.

CHAPTER FIVE

LEO THE SERVANT

The next morning I moved into Wanda's place in La Jolla. It was a rather elaborate residence up near Mount Soledad. Not quite a mansion but a far cry from the bourgeois bungalow I was living in. The Manor had a large living room, two bedrooms and three bathrooms, an enormous dining room that could seat a dozen guests easily, and a banquet-sized kitchen.

There was a two-car garage at the side and a swimming pool and cabaña in the rear.

Above the garage were the servants' quarters. The quarters consisted of two rooms. One was a rather cramped little space sparsely furnished with an army cot, a shabby dresser and a decrepit table. It had an attached bath and a tiny closet, both of which appeared to be afterthoughts.

The second room above the garage, also originally meant to be another servants' quarters, was twice the size of the previous room.

When Wanda showed it to me, she said, "And this, Leo, is Limbo."

One glance confirmed the function of the room. It was smaller than the Purgatory down at Fourth and Market. But it was similarly equipped with pulleys, crosses, spanking benches and most of the other instruments of torture that graced our previous chamber.

"How do you like it, Leo?" Wanda asked in those sweet tones of hers that beguiled me so.

"I love it, Wanda," I replied truthfully.

I felt comfortable addressing her by her given name.

"For the remainder of our stay in San Diego," she told me. "You are to be my obsequious personal servant. And as such, you will always address me as 'Ma'am,' 'Madam' or 'Madame' depending on the circumstances. I shall address you by your last name, Messick. And when I am displeased I may resort to calling you 'Messy.'

"Your quarters shall be the adjacent room. It is, as you have observed, Spartan in keeping with your humble status. You will discover that it is equipped with a buzzer system which I control.

"When I give a double buzz to your quarters, I will expect you to immediately drop everything you are doing and report to me in the Manor.

"Do you understand?"

"Yes, Madam," I replied.

She gave me a jolting slap to the face.

"Did I mention that you will always respond with an obeisant bow?" she asked.

"Thank you for informing me of that courtesy, Madam," I told her with a bow that quite pleased me.

Wanda handed me two keys.

"Here, Messick," she said. "One of these will gain you entrance to the Manor. The other key is to your quarters.

"You may go now to your quarters. In the room's closet you will find your livery. You will attire yourself only in servants' clothes of my choosing for as long as you serve me.

"I will buzz you there when I have further need of your presence."

She stopped talking, looked at me and waited for a response.

I had no idea what to say and stood there with what I suppose was a foolish look on my face.

With a quick flick of her hand she gave me a double slap to the face, with each side of her hand.

"Don't just stand there like an idiot when you perceive that I have given you an order, Nincompoop," she thundered.

"Do I have to write a script for you? You bow, you say 'Very good, Madam,' and get on with the job. Do you understand?"

I bowed. I scraped. I ventured, "I regret my ineptitude, Ma'am. Very good. I will attend to your wishes immediately…" And before she could administer another slap, I rapidly added "…Madam."

I was quite proud of myself. I felt I was learning fast.

I stepped aside so Madame could get past me to make her stately departure from Limbo.

I then followed her.

I thought perhaps the key to my quarters might lock the Limbo room after me. It did.

I treasured the burning tingles on my cheeks from Madam's slaps as I proceeded on to my quarters to see what 'livery' awaited me in my closet.

I re-entered my Spartan room and proceeded directly to my closet.

I opened the closet door and was presented with three satin suits styled along eighteenth century lines. One suit was black, another robin's egg blue and the other pink. The jackets were cut in a style favored by George Washington, with lace cuffs. The satin breeches were tight fitting. Each suit was accompanied by a silk cravat of matching color.

I tried on the black livery which fit me perfectly.

Although the outfit was quite elegant, and appropriate for wearing at the Manor, I felt that if I were to wear it out in public I would be an object of derision.

Then I realized that was the exact purpose Wanda had in mind. The attire was intended not only to reinforce my subservience to her. It was additionally intended to humiliate me in public.

Just the thing for a masochist like me.

I was in the process of admiring the way the tight satin breeches showed off my bulge to advantage when the buzzer sounded its summons.

Wanda's previous orders rang perfectly in my mind.

"When I give a double buzz to your quarters, I will expect you to immediately drop everything you are doing and report to me in the Manor."

I smoothed my bulge, rushed out of the room, scrambled down the steps, ran to the Manor, let myself in the back door and hustled around the place to locate where my mistress was located.

I hurried to the living room and found her seated at the coffee table.

"You rang, Madam?" I asked as I bowed in her direction.

"Coffee and croissants, Messick," she ordered.

Now, what the Hell was I supposed to do? How was I going to whump up coffee? And where were there any damned croissants in the place?

"Very good, Madam," I said as I bowed myself out of the room and hurried to the kitchen.

And there I was surprised and delighted to find…guess who?

There stood Rachel, decked out in a maid's outfit.

Yes, the Rachel, the majestic lady with the mahogany colored skin whom I had encountered over in Purgatory.

My Willie did a little quick-step when I saw her. For I remembered the way I had licked and kissed every surface and cranny of that voluptuous body the previous evening.

The blip at my fly did not go un-noticed by the very observant Rachel.

She gave me a quick lesson on how to grind the coffee beans that were sitting on the counter. Then, she taught me how to operate the espresso machine to brew coffee exactly as Madam desired it.

She assembled two croissants with butter and jam and showed me how to set up the tray correctly with the coffee service.

"I won't always be around here to help you, Messy," she smiled. "You'd better remember this routine if you know what's good for you."

Oh, I would remember all right.

When I returned to the living room I said, "Your coffee, Madame."

Although I made the required bow, Madam was not looking, so the gesture went wasted.

Madam merely pointed at the coffee table in front of her to demonstrate where she expected me to set up the service.

I complied.

Madam took a trial sip of the coffee and then buttered and nibbled on a croissant.

Finally, she deigned to look at me.

"I have an errand I want you to run, Messick," she informed me.

"Yes, Madam," I responded with my bow.

"I want you to go to Victoria's Secret, the lingerie shop in Mission Valley."

I knew the boutique. It sells quite a sexy line of women's underwear. I had never been inside the store but had often ogled the scantily clad manikins in the window display.

"You are to buy a pair of pink panties there," she continued. "The more shockingly seductive the better"

Oh, how I longed to have my mistress wearing such undies. Particularly while she spanked me to a frenzy.

"I want you to purchase a brassiere there as well. Be sure to tell the clerk you want one that will enhance the sexiness of the panties."

I pictured Wanda in such provocative underclothes. I could not control a blip in my dong.

I hoped Madam caught sight of it.

"Yes, Ma'am," I responded bowing. "But I am afraid I do not know what sizes you wear."

"You do not need to know that, Messick," Wanda replied firmly. "The articles are not meant to fit me. I am not the one who will be wearing them."

I was puzzled at first. Then it dawned on me that she was buying the unmentionables for Rachel.

While I was cogitating on how splendid Rachel would look in the sexy underclothes, Wanda sprang the blockbuster on me.

"You are to buy the articles in a size that will fit *you*. You must tell the clerk that *you* are buying them to wear yourself. Make that point quite clear to the saleslady. Do you understand?"

"Yes, Madam," I replied with a touch of a grimace. "As you please."

She dismissed me and I left the Manor to go outside to where my aged Honda Civic was parked at the curb.

Wanda's Mercedes was parked in the garage. But I did not dare even suggest that she allow me to drive it on my errand.

When I got to the mall, I was filled with apprehension. What would the saleslady at Victoria's Secret think of me? I had grown used to humiliation over the years. I'd thrived on it as a matter of fact. Those of us who are addicted to pain relish psychological punishment as well as its physical manifestation. But to be taken for a transvestite, that was something I was not sure I could deal with very well.

Yet, my goddess had directed me to purchase panties and a bra for myself. So that was what I was about to transact.

I stood outside the boutique admiring the window display as I always did when at the mall. The lingerie modeled by the manikin caused a jolt to my gonads. I could imagine my svelte Wanda scantily attired in those pink duds.

Ah! Glorious!

A second image popped unexpectedly into my mind. The full-bodied Rachel appeared there in that same erotic garb.

Oops! I sprang a hardon and would have to walk it off before entering Victoria's Secret.

A ten minute stroll through the mall was sufficient to do the trick.

When I arrived back in front of Victoria's Secret, I did not dare ogle the display window again. My imagination did not need another romp with its unintended consequences.

An attractive young saleslady approached me when I entered the boutique. She appeared quite comfortable greeting a young gentleman wearing a silk cravat and attired in a black satin suit with lace cuffs.

"May I help you?" she inquired.

"Yes," I answered feeling a blush assaulting my cheeks.

"I would like to purchase the pink panties and bra displayed in the window."

The sweet young thing evidenced no surprise.

"Ah, yes," she said. "The ensemble is called the Du Berry. It is quite popular. What size would you like?"

This was the hard part. I had to unclasp my teeth to respond.

"Whatever size would fit me," I blurted out.

The young lady was unfazed. Clearly I was not a freak customer in her eyes.

Transvestites must not be uncommon customers in that boutique because she looked me over professionally, asked me to wait while she put together a package she assured me would fit, and smiled sweetly as I paid for the pink items.

I knew I would never ever be uncomfortable purchasing underclothes at Victoria's Secret again should the unlikely occasion ever arise again. The employees welcome men who are there to purchase sexy underclothes for themselves.

When I returned to the Manor, Madam was in the dining room enjoying dessert and coffee.

Rachel entered asking whether Madam wanted a refill of coffee.

"No, thank you, Rachel," she was told.

"I have quite enough left. You may leave now. And your services will not be required again until tomorrow when you arrive to prepare luncheon. I will be going out to dinner this evening and Messick will take care of all my needs until then."

"Very good, Ma'am," Rachel answered as she bowed her way out of the room and back into the kitchen.

At that moment I figured out the servant set-up in the place. Clearly Rachel came to the Manor to prepare the noontime and evening meals and to do the grocery shopping.

It was my function to take care of all the other duties that Madam's whims might dictate.

I assumed that Rachel would leave morning croissants for me to serve Madam in the morning. That assumption proved to be correct.

And as to my own nutritional needs? I knew that I would simply have to scrounge around for leftovers.

I waited, standing at attention with my package under my left arm as Madam finished off the remains of her lemon meringue pie and sipped the last drops of her coffee.

When she had patted her lips and sighed, she rewarded me by glancing in my direction.

"Yes, Messick?" she asked.

I bowed and replied:

"I have returned from the mall, Ma'am, with the items you sent me to purchase."

"Of course," she answered with a yawn. "Open the packages and let me see whether you botched the job or not."

Her supercilious tone lit a fire in my heart. That woman was truly a mistress of contempt. Just what I thrive on.

I removed the panties and bra from the box and handed them to her.

She inspected them carefully and laughed heartily.

"Oh, Messick," she chortled. "You actually did something right for a change. You will look darling in this attire.

"After I give you some further instructions, I will want you to take these pink items right up to your quarters and put them on.

"I have an additional buzzer code for you when you are in your quarters. A triple buzz will mean 'put on your pink lingerie and proceed directly to Limbo.'

"Do you suppose you can manage to remember that?"

"Yes, Ma'am," I retorted with a bow. "Very good. I feel sure I can manage to remember all that."

She arose from her chair holding the lingerie in her left hand. As she extended the items out toward me, she gave me a resounding slap to my face.

"Smart Alec remarks like that are most unbecoming," she snarled.

"I am so sorry, Madam," I replied. "I did not mean to offend."

Slightly dizzy from the whack to my face, I bowed out of the room and returned to my quarters.

The clerk at the store was right. The panties fit me fine around the waist. They pressed my pecker tight against my balls, of course. Those panties provided no give whatsoever for the masculine bulge

I experimented some and found that my prick fit most comfortably within the nylon and lace constriction if I wore it pointing up rather than down. And, I reflected that, when I had a hardon while wearing those panties, I would not be able to manage getting it pointed up the right way if it were not already oriented North.

The bra, however, turned out to be no problem. The brassiere the young lady had chosen for me was designed for a very flat-chested woman. Or, of course, equally for a transvestite man.

I had heard the expression "training bra." I supposed my titless condition warranted "training."

Oops! The buzzer buzzed thrice.

It was show time!

Clad only in my bra, panties and slippers, I left my quarters.

My first problem was that the walkway from my quarters to Limbo was all exterior. That is to say, anyone down at street-level who chanced to be looking up would be greeted with the sight of a young man attired in sexy female lingerie walking along an outside passageway.

And that ridiculous personage would be…me.

I covered the distance as quickly as I could. I was somewhat out of breath when I paused outside the door to Limbo.

Who cares what a nosey neighbor might think about me in girlie underclothes up there on the second floor?

I would gladly walk over hot coals to get to my Venus.

I opened the door and there she was. My Venus in Leather.

Yes, she was wearing her leather cat suit and cap. She stood tall in her stiletto platform boots with her cat-o'-nine-tails trailing down from her left hand.

The sight overwhelmed me and threw my prick into an instant woodie. *Thank God I was wearing my dick upright when I entered the room.*

"My, but you *do* look cute, Pansy," she greeted me.

So there it was. In that guise I was going to be called "Pansy."

My masculine identity was about to be tested.

Mortifying. Embarrassing. Soul wrenching.

My Venus really knew how to get a man where it hurts.

Deep down into his deepest manly core.

She perceived that I had swallowed my new identity as Pansy. Her tone changed abruptly to one of righteous indignation.

"You have been harboring indecent thoughts, you naughty little girl. Haven't you?" she accused.

I was not sure how to address her. Who was she in this new relationship she had devised? Surely not Wanda. Venus did not seem an appropriate match as disciplinarian for little Pansy either. Ma'am, Madam and Madame would be clumsy fits at best.

Not knowing what else to do, I threw myself down at her feet and kissed her boots.

"I am all confused," I sobbed. "I am a very stupid little girl and have lost my Mommy. Will *you* be my Mommy?"

"You poor, stupid child," she answered. "Don't you recognize your Aunt Domina? Your Mommy died. She died of grief when she learned about the unchaste thoughts you harbor in that wicked little head of yours.

"How can you possibly atone for such turpitude?"

So. It was to be the punishing auntie and the naughty little girl who would be the protagonists in this venue. I had learned a lot from "Auntie" Gertrude and Aunt Sarah about the lavish thrill of pain and subjection. I felt sure that "Aunt Domina" would employ just the right techniques for dealing with the recalcitrant Pansy.

We girls surely give more vent to tears, screams and giggles than stupid boys do. This could be a lark.

In answer to Auntie's pregnant question, I answered:

"Oh, Auntie! I have been a very wicked little girl. I deserve a good, sound spanking."

It seemed that Auntie could not agree more.

And, it just so happened that a spanking bench was one of the furnishings of the room.

There was no surprise there. I had noticed it with happy anticipation when I was first shown the room.

"Get yourself over there, then, you little hoyden," she ordered. "And Auntie will teach you a lesson you will not soon forget."

I was more than ready to learn that lesson, I assure you.

I pranced over to that bench with a girlish traipse. I placed my feet in the outermost slots and leaned over the top plank to reach the holding bars down at floor level.

My panty-clad derrière was delicately poised for the warranted castigation of a morally incensed auntie.

Auntie came around the bench to show me the instrument of correction she had chosen to employ.

The effort to raise my head to observe the object put a very uncomfortable strain on my neck and back.

My discomfort did not appear to disturb my dear newly-acquired relative.

"My beloved nephew, Rupert, is a member of a fraternity at the university," she informed me. "He brought his dear auntie this delightful paddle. It is called a 'frat paddle.' Note the holes drilled randomly about its surface. And the little wooden pyramids scattered about its business side. The effect of the holes and the protrusions on a darling little behind are just precious."

The paddle was a sight to behold. About a foot and a half long, half a foot wide, and perhaps two inches thick, it was a whacker that carried an awesome authority. I believed my Auntie Domina could out swat any frat-boy in the land with it.

When Auntie had done intimidating me with the goddam paddle, she retreated to the other side of the bench to demonstrate the malevolence of its application.

I knew the sheer quality of my panties would not give me much protection against the spirited use Auntie Domina meant to use against my tightly stretched glutes.

I heard the swish as she extended her arm to maximize the swing she was taking.

For her benefit, I whimpered.

I knew she loved to hear me whimper.

But my whimpers were not emitted only for her delectation. For the expectation of a painful blow always elicited a primal response of some kind even from the lips of a devoted masochist like me.

Strange, isn't it?

Oh, how pleased I was with myself that I had prepared myself ahead of time by wearing my prick upright beneath my panties.

For when that vicious paddle made stinging contact with my ass, the pain shot from my butt cheeks right into my tucked in balls and threw my dong into an immediate vibrant boner.

With each enthusiastic swat from Auntie, the pain enhanced the pressure at my groin.

By the twentieth application of the instrument, I knew that pre-cum was gracing my piss-hole.

At twenty-five strokes, I was emptying fountains of jism into those sweet pink panties of mine.

My whimpers had morphed into sighs of ecstasy and Auntie's breathing had reached aerobic stages.

Both of us were in a state of euphoria.

Auntie pulled down my panties from the back and I must have satisfied her sense of accomplishment when she saw the bleeding welts she had raised . For she pulled the underwear back up over my ass and told me to unfold myself from the fricking bench.

When I turned around, she saw how soggy the front of the panties were with sticky, noisome cum, and she actually smiled.

"Well, Pansy," she smiled. "Aren't you a messy little pervert."

The way she said "Pansy" and the statement of the word "pervert" truly made me feel like a catamite. For the first time I felt ashamed on account of my appearance.

I actually blushed. Which sent Auntie into a convulsion of laughter.

She was laughing *at* me.

Degraded, I knew I was pleasing her in my ludicrous condition.

I thought that would be the end of the session.

But, as I had so often done before, I had underestimated my evil Venus.

"Now, Snarf," she said to me. "Take off those pink panties, hold them up to your nose and breathe in that male scent that turns you on so."

I took off the panties, held them up to my nose and inhaled.

I gagged. I could not help it.

"No, no," Auntie chided. "You love the smell too much to simply take dainty whiffs of that lovely cum. I want to see you get your sweet little nose right down into it."

I want to tell you. That was worse. Lots worse. But I obeyed her and got my nose right down into that splotch of ripe cum anyway.

I was afraid I was going to puke.

But...I managed to plunge my nose into the mess.

"Yummy, yummy, yum," Auntie teased. "How our little Pansy loves her cum cocktail.

"All right, then, Pansy darling. I want you to lick up some of your favorite queer delight. Lick the rest of the goop out of those panties."

I licked. And I puked. Right there on the floor.

Auntie rocked with glee.

"You'll find a mop and pail over in the corner of the room, Pansy," she directed. "I'll just sit in the comfy chair over there by the wall and watch you clean up your mess.

"No wonder I have to call you 'Messy,' you degenerate!"

My Venus was, indeed, an evil goddess. She loved to punish her votaries as wickedly as she knew how, both physically and psychologically.

God! How I loved that celestial being.

When I had completely cleaned up the mess I had left on the floor, I crawled over to where Auntie Domina was sitting and licked her boots. I tongued every inch of leather until it shone resplendently.

She explored the boots carefully and declared them adequately polished when I had completed the task.

My cloddish behavior for having sullied the floor apparently was magnanimously forgiven.

"What a pleasant little diversion we have enjoyed here in our pantomime of the naughty little girl child being punished for her transgressions," she intoned.

I nodded my toadying agreement.

"It is time now for us to take a new tack in our relationship," she continued.

"It is all very well that you obey my every command and direction here in the privacy of my home. But that is scarcely warrant for me to accept your subservience.

"You must prove your abject devotion to me out in the great world as well.

"I need to see how you take to being my menial servant here in San Diego before we can even consider leaving for Florence."

Ah, Florence! To worship Venus in Florence! What a vision!

For the next month, Wanda *did* the town. She took in plays and concerts. She visited museums and parks. She breakfasted, lunched and dined in the finest cafés, restaurants and bistros. She attended parties, balls and fiestas.

And she was attended at all these events by her obsequious self-effacing factotum who was always decked out in his ridiculous eighteenth century satin livery, black, blue or pink.

Of course, I never sat with her at the eateries. I attended her as she sat or stood and then returned to a spot by the wall where the serving staff observed me with annoyance.

At functions like parties, I brought her in, took care of her wraps, and found somewhere in the shadows to stand while being observed by the merrymakers with poorly concealed amusement.

The opportunities to display myself subserviently in every possible social situation abounded.

My status was most embarrassing when one of my friends or acquaintances from my previous life spotted me. After all, I had lived in San Diego County for most of my life. I truly had an abundance of friends, co-workers, schoolmates and casual acquaintances. It was inevitable that I would be run into not infrequently while my Venus was lavishly doing the town.

But it was the rare acquaintance who felt comfortable stopping to exchange a word with me. And, likewise, I hardly felt like discussing with them what I was doing in my satin outfit toadying to the gorgeous blonde lady who was always sparkling in the swing of things.

When I had satisfied Wanda that I could be a subservient enough valet to her as she gadded about in town, she turned the screws up tighter for me.

One balmy evening, she went to dinner at Valentine's, a fashionable sidewalk café on Fifth Avenue in the Gaslamp Quarter.

I remember she had ordered sweetbreads prepared in sherry as her main course. What she enjoyed as her soup and salad courses I do not recall at the moment.

As she was eating the sweetbreads, she was discreetly flirting with a handsome Latino gentleman who was sitting two tables away.

I was, as was my custom, standing in a corner watching my lady to determine whether there was any way I could be of service to her. My stomach was rumbling and my mouth salivating since I had not had a thing to eat since breakfast and sweetbreads are one of my all-time favorite dishes.

Madame's flirtations were, of course, discreet and coy. Only a gentleman schooled in the subtleties of urbane coquetry would have been aware of her glances, the way she patted her lips with her napkin or her cunning weight shifts in her chair.

The gentleman showed the same sophistication in his responses. His smile, the lift of his eyebrows and the manner in which he arranged the napkin on his lap indicated that he understood her flirtiness.

Madame shrugged her shoulders with the motion that I knew to be her summons.

I glided to stand at her side.

"As I am leaving this café, I wish you to place my assignation card on the gentleman's table," she ordered me.

Ah, yes. The assignation card.

It was a small card on which was embossed only her first name and the address of our Paradise at Fourth and Market.

If the gentleman were so disposed, he could send an invitation to her at that venue.

Madame, of course, was not so vulgar as to reveal her home address or telephone number to a stranger.

She had revealed to the gentleman a manner in which she could be contacted. And it was all handled with her customary elegance and discretion.

Who knew what action the Latin caballero might take?

Two days later, Madam sent me Downtown to see if any mail had been delivered to her Paradise address.

I retrieved an envelope there, which I brought back to my goddess' La Jolla home.

She was kind enough to share the invitation enclosed in the envelope with me.

It was a formal invitation from a Señor Atilio Ruiz Solórzano requesting the honor of Señorita Wanda's company at an intimate *diner à deux* at his residence in the Coronado Cays at eight p.m. the following Saturday.

The residence was on Turtle Road.

Talk about a classy address! I knew the Cays. And I knew that all the homes on Turtle Road had their own individual yacht berths. The lady had an eye for class.

She sent me to the señor's mansion in the Coronado Cays with a formal response accepting the invitation.

On Saturday, attired in my pink livery, I chauffeured Madam to the Coronado Cays in the Mercedes.

I had no sooner pulled up to the curb in front of Señor Ruiz Solórzano's magnificent home than a butler came out the door and was opening the rear door of the car before I could even budge.

Like a good chauffeur, I sat stiffly, facing straight ahead until Madam had been escorted to the door.

I looked towards that door to see the Señor kiss her hand. The butler then exited, closed the door behind him and came out to the Mercedes.

In Spanish-accented but perfect American speech, he came around to my side of the car.

"Hi, Sport," he said. "I'm Tony. Who are you?"

I got out of the car and shook his hand.

"I'm Leo, Madam's drudge and flunky," I told him.

"You can leave the Mercedes parked out here on the street if you want. It's a safe neighborhood," he advised me.

"Come on around to the servants' quarters. You'll probably have a long wait. El Señor is a horny bastard and he gives his ladies a nice long ride in the sack."

I knew I was going to like this guy.

When we got to the common room for the staff, Tony introduced me to a few of Atilio's crew who were gathered there. A buffet was set up and the folks were eating.

"We'll be in and out of here as we go to serve the *jefe* and your lady," Tony told me.

"Help yourself to the food and drink. Make yourself at home. Feel free to tune in anything you want on the TV. It'll be a long wait for you. I told you our *jefe* takes his time when he's entertaining *las chulitas*."

Tony left me then.

The food and drink were excellent. Servants paraded in and out as they went to do their thing. They pretty much left me alone as I watched Saturday Night Live and the rest of the TV offerings I like.

I'd finally dozed off. It was a lot later when Tony tapped me on the shoulder.

"Hey, Sport," he said. "Better wake up. You're wanted in the master's bedroom."

In Atilio's bedroom? What the Hell?

Tony led me through the lavishly furnished and decorated mansion. It made Wanda's place look like a dump in comparison.

This Atilio was clearly one very rich dude.

When we got to the master bedroom door, Tony smiled. Or was it a smirk?

Hard to tell.

"Good luck, Sport," he told me. "El Señor has a few bizarre tastes and habits. Be cool!"

He knocked on the door.

A masculine voice from inside the room said, "Enter."

So, enter I did. Not without a certain amount of trepidation.

When I walked into the room, Madame and Atilio were standing next to a bed that was not standard, queen size or even king size. Is there such a thing as an emperor size? Or master-of-the-universe size?

The bedroom itself was enormous. And the bed filled three-fourths of the space.

It was, I realized, not a bed but an entire playing field.

And the game my lady and her swain had been playing appeared to be approaching the fourth quarter.

Madame was attired in a pink silk negligee. The pink, I was distressed to note, was the exact shade as the livery I was wearing.

El Señor was wearing a lavender and black colored robe made of a transparent material I did not recognize.

"Oh, Messick," Madame said in a haughty tone when I appeared.

"El Señor and I are about to engage in a finale to our festivities.

"We are both in need of stimulation, since we have expended an immense amount of libidinous energy thus far this evening.

"We have replenished our resources with large quantities of oysters and Grande Dame.

"But we have come to the point where our amatory reserves require an expenditure of a touch of sadistic frivolity.

"Remove your clothing, Messick, and take your position at the whipping post."

A whipping post had become a familiar sight to me since I had made Wanda's acquaintance.

And disrobing to receive whippings had certainly been part of my life for as long as I could remember.

However, getting bound to a post and being whipped while naked under the cruel eye of Señor Atilio added a dimension to my abject disciplinary subjection that was not particularly welcome.

"Yes, Madam," I answered with a wrenching shudder." As you wish."

The two lovers stood there eyeing me with lascivious grins as I removed every stitch of clothing I had on.

As I looked up after I had removed my shoes I saw that the master and mistress had removed their clothing as well and were standing there bare-ass nude.

Each had a whip in hand. I had acquired a full education about whips in my time. So I immediately was able to spot the variety of each of the instruments I knew would soon be inflicted on my skin.

The flagellum in Madame's hand was clearly a snakewhip. The whip's plaited belly gives it a pointed accuracy. It rolls out perfectly straight with a lead shot bag at its business end.

El Señor's whip was a signalwhip. It takes a sharp eye to note the difference between a signalwhip and a snakewhip. Both have the lead at the tip, of course. But a signalwhip is more flexible and more suited to slashing than to stinging.

The appearance of the two whips is similar. The type of pain inflicted to the recipient's back, however, varies excruciatingly .

I knew I would be having myself a time as my host and hostess reinforced their libidos at the expense of my exposed back.

Without having to be told, I walked over to the post and dutifully clasped my arms about its circumference.

Atilio met me there promptly with a pair of handcuffs and snapped them about my wrists.

Thinking about the whipping I was about to receive from Wanda and Atilio caused me to spring a boner that pressed deliciously against the post.

Atilio took note of my reaction, smiled and winked at Wanda.

Oh what a time that happy couple was about to enjoy.

The first attack came from Wanda's whip. How did I know? Because it was a piercing sharp sting of a lead-tipped thong that struck me square on my sixth thoracic vertebra. Man, does that ever hurt! It clearly was delivered by a snakewhip. And Wanda had early taught me that the sixth thoracic vertebra is the most sensitive nerve center of the entire backbone.

Some three seconds later a second strike landed on the identical spot.

I could not control myself. I screamed at the top of my voice. The pain was deadly. It was exquisite.

At the same moment, my Venus let out a venomous curse in Surinamese Dutch.

I had barely regained the ability to breathe again when a pain coursed across my back from my left shoulder to my right buttock.

There was no question about the source of that slash. It was the leaden tip of a signalwhip wielded by an expert. The sensation was like having a rusty knife viciously flay me. Atilio had demonstrated to his South American sweetheart that he was not to be outdone in cruel expertise.

I yelped, which brought a volley of male laughter from behind me.

The laughter was followed by a second application of the signalwhip, this time burning a trail from my right shoulder blade to my left ass-cheek.

Atilio's Spanish language curse and chortle nearly drowned out my agonized cry.

I cannot tell you how many strokes I endured before I fainted.

What I *can* tell you is how many ejaculations I experienced before I expired.

In my agonized ecstasy I came seven different times. The last three orgasms were dry-cums. But wet or dry, each orgasm sent my soul reeling into a heaven or nirvana.

The dual flagellation was one of the most spiritual experiences of my life.

I was not aware of Atilio removing my manacles. I awoke from my oblivion sprawled out on the floor at the foot of the post noting nothing but the splotches and scent of my jism on that post.

As I resumed more and more consciousness, I felt a severe kick to my ribs.

That bastard Atilio had gone to the trouble of putting a boot on his right foot with the express purpose of kicking me.

"Get up off my floor, you filthy punk," he shouted at me. "Your mistress and I have need of you over at the bed. *Andale, hijo de la chingada. Pronto! Pronto!"*

When I had managed to roll myself over onto my hands and knees, I managed to grunt out the words I knew were appropriate to my status:

"Gracias, Señor."

In response he gave me a sturdy kick in the ass that sent me sprawling.

Atilio's robust laugh punctuated my collapse.

By the time I managed to pull myself up into standing position, I noted that the son of a bitch had removed his boot and was now barefoot and bare assed.

He and my Venus were clasped in an embrace on that gigantic bed.

I did not need to be told that I was expected to trot over to the bed and provide whatever service might be demanded of me.

"Oh, there you are, Messick," my mistress noted.

"Señor Atilio likes to have his balls gently held while he fucks."

"Climb up here on the bed and fondle his '*huevos*' while he services me."

Atilio proceeded to mount Wanda.

I placed myself behind the couple and managed to perform the function my lady demanded of me.

It was the most humiliating thing I had ever done.

When the couple ended their coitus in a shrieking convulsion, I released that fucker's balls and fell, again, senseless off the bed and onto the floor.

When I awoke, Wanda and Atilio were no longer in the room.

Tony was wiping my forehead with a damp cloth.

"Are you all right, Sport?" he asked me.

"I told you the *jefe* had a few bizarre tastes, didn't I?"

I agreed that he had so told me. And that he was certainly right about what he had said.

Tony applied salve to the slashes and pits on my back that gave testimony to the beating I had suffered at the hands of my Venus and her Adonis.

He helped me get back into my clothes and offered me a couple of welcome shots of tequila.

When he helped me out of the mansion and to the Mercedes, Wanda was already sitting in the back seat awaiting my arrival.

I got into the driver's seat and chauffeured her home.

Before Wanda dismissed me to my quarters for the night, she smiled very sweetly at me.

"You demonstrated your abject devotion to me this evening rather well," she allowed.

"You have shown that you adore being beaten, kicked, demeaned and humiliated, as a good slave should.

"So, tomorrow morning, return to your home in Ocean Beach, close it up and return here with your passport.

"For you have passed the domestic servants' test. We leave next week for Florence. Where you must prove to me you can demean yourself adequately in that more sophisticated urbane setting."

Florence!

I could hardly wait.

CHAPTER SIX

FLORENTINE FLAGELLATIONS

When we arrived at Los Angeles International Airport, I was dressed in my robin-egg blue livery. Wanda had told me to leave all my other outer clothing behind in Ocean Beach. I was to wear only her livery from then on.

Once inside the terminal, she handed me my plane ticket. It was for coach class.

I saw that hers was for business class.

Of course, both tickets were for the same flight, Los Angeles to Rome. Our seating would simply be in accordance with our respective classes, mistress and servant.

At the time, Wanda gave me a pocket-sized English-Italian dictionary. It proved very useful once we got to Florence.

While we were waiting to board, Wanda reminded me again of the basic rules that would prevail while we were abroad.

There would be no form of familiarity at all between us, of course. I was not ever to speak to her unless previously permitted.

I was not to address her any more as "Ma'am" "Madame," or "Madam." It was to be Signorina, Madama, or, on occasion, La Contessa.

I would have in my possession only sufficient money to make phone calls except when she specifically entrusted me with cash or with a special debit card in order to make specific purchases for her.

And I was to be addressed by her during our Italian stay as Fido.

Fido? I guess that *told me something.*

When we arrived at Leonardo da Vinci-Fiumicino Airport, I gathered our luggage while La Contessa was making contact with the limousine driver who had been awaiting our arrival.

When we were seated in the limo, the chauffeur carried on a short conversation with Madama. Then we were on our way to Florence, some one hundred seventy-five miles away.

Four hours later, our chauffeur brought us to the door of La Contessa's hotel in Florence, the Castello Cavalcanti al Duomo on the Via dei Servi.

As indicated by its name, the hotel is actually a castle. It was built in 1300 as home and fortress for the Cavalcanti family who were leaders of the White Guelph political party in the Fourteenth Century. I do not know enough about Florentine history to tell why they needed a large fortified castle in the center of the city. But, they did.

And today, the damned place has been turned into the grandest hotel I've ever seen.

No one is even allowed to get through the door of the place except registered guests. Or invited guests of a guest. Or, like the chauffeur and me, employees or servants of a guest. You get the picture.

La Contessa swept into the palatial lobby followed by the chauffeur and me lugging her luggage.

I have no idea what that enormous room was used for back in the Fifteenth Century. Today it is partly the reception center for the exclusive hotel among other things.

Every wall of the place is covered with frescos depicting scenes from Dante's Inferno. The ceiling is painted with scenes from Dante's life.

Damndest place you've ever seen.

I'm not going to go on and on about the Castello Cavalcanti. The whole place is like some kind of museum-cum-hotel. Except that you cannot even get in to see the museum unless you're staying there or otherwise permitted in.

Although much of the décor was updated during the Renaissance, one room has been kept pretty much intact as it was when constructed. That room is the subterranean torture chamber.

I'll tell you more about that later.

We got my Wanda, a.k.a. Madama, a.k.a. La Contessa all set up in her sumptuous room. Then Madama, the chauffeur and I got back out into the limousine to take me to the lodgings my mistress had provided for me.

I was to stay in a very humble albergo some fifteen hundred yards from the Castello. That is fifteen hundred yards as the crow flies. Somewhat farther, I assure you, as the streets wind.

It is called the Albergo Grosso, located on Borgo Pinti.

It is a pretty run down hostelry. Quite unprepossessing from the outside. And fairly depressing once you get inside.

The wallpaper is blistered. The furniture is decrepit. There is one bathroom to serve the eight guest rooms.

The best quality of the place is Signora Pucci. The proprietress. She was chubby and smiley. And, although she neither spoke nor understood English, by speaking Spanish and using my pocket Italian dictionary, I was able to communicate satisfactorily enough with her.

There was a telephone in the Signora's living room which could be used by the guests for two euros a call (incoming or outgoing). That telephone would be the means for Madama to contact me during our Florentine stay.

La Contessa and her chauffeur left me at my albergo to settle in.

She had not told me when she would want me to attend her next, so I was pretty much stuck where she had left me.

Actually, the Albergo Grosso was not all that much more tawdry than the Pancho Villa Hotel I had stayed in in Zihuatanejo. And Signora Pucci was pleasant enough to be with. It turned out that she was susceptible to a bit of hanky-panky. Well, actually, quite a bit more than a bit.

My problem was that I was stuck with having to stay inside the joint all the time awaiting La Contessa's telephonic summons.

Back at the Pancho Villa, I had been able to come and go pretty much as I pleased. At the albergo I was somewhat of a prisoner.

But, on the plus side, Signora Pucci, who encouraged me to call her Rosina, was more than pleasant to be with.

Within hours we had passed from a few furtive kisses to explorations of each other's bodily parts.

Before I left Florence, I had taught her to take pleasure in spanking me with her fine Italian hand and in beating me with her broom handle and fly swatter.

But my intimacies with Rosina Pucci are not really a part of the tale I want to tell here. So I leave that mini-romantic tale for you to work out in your own imagination.

Towards evening, while Rosina and I were enjoying a salad and a batch of her cheese ravioli accompanied by a hearty *vino da tavola* the phone rang.

It was a summons from La Contessa to get right over to the Castello in my black livery.

Even though Rosina and I had become quite physically involved while I was a guest in her albergo, I always paid her the two euros per phone call.

After all. We both understood, business is business.

So, I paid her the two euros, rushed up to my room, donned my black outfit and hoofed it through the streets of Florence to attend to my mistress.

I got to her suite in about twenty minutes.

The Contessa expressed annoyance that it had taken me so long to get to her after her call. I apologized and that seemed to satisfy her because she did not slap me.

Better luck next time.

She told me she was going to Ristorante Raffaelo and that this would be the first real test of my subservience in the Old World.

"Unlike your barbaric people in San Diego, Europeans, and Florentines in particular, appreciate a servant who is completely obsequious. Entire volumes were written by famous authors like Machiavelli on how toadying a servant should behave. The distinction between servant and slave was blurred by everyone back then. And still is by people of distinction.

"So here, in this truly cultivated city, expect to be treated far, far less kindly by me than you were in the New World.

"Our stay here is your opportunity to demonstrate that you are fit to be a real slave if I should choose to allow you to accompany me back to Surinam eventually."

I guess I was being warned to be my particularly smarmy self.

Following this little lecture we left the Castello and took a taxi to the Via dei Magazzini.

The Ristorante Raffaello was founded in 1666 and has been dispensing Tuscan cuisine there since its inception.

When we stepped in, I was struck by the fact that the interior was illuminated only by candlelight. The flickering light that was shed on the glasses, silverware and plates that adorn the antique tables scintillated reflections everywhere.

The ceiling is a vault ornamented with elaborate frescos representing meats, fruit and vegetables of all sorts.

A string quartet was playing Baroque music. And the wait staff was outfitted in suits not too unlike my own livery.

The Contessa was seated by the maitre d' at a table that gave her a perfect view of the room. But, more important, it gave the other guests a perfect view of her.

I was happy to discover that I was not the only lackey in the room. An entire wall was occupied by servants of the diners. There were even a few who spoke English. When I asked around, I discovered that the diners included rich Americans, English Milords, French aristocrats and multi-lingual diners galore.

I was standing at the flunky wall next to a guy named Gaylord . The guy informed me that the curtained doors along one of the walls led to private rooms for discreet couples. (Whatever that meant.)

When my Contessa was seated, and had her napkin placed in her lap, a chap with a big bottle hustled over to her table and poured her a glass of Prosecco. I could tell it was a white bubbly wine.

She took a sip and shrugged a shoulder – her signal for me to hurry over to her table.

I bent over to inquire what she wanted.

She slapped me smartly on the cheek.

I realized she had hit me only to make a statement to her fellow diners. I never figured out just what that statement was. But I bowed politely and said, "Very good, Contessa," just loud enough for those at near-by tables to hear.

Then I returned to the flunky wall.

The next thing I noticed was a waiter pushing a salad cart over to her table.

While he very flamboyantly tossed an elaborate salad before her eyes, she was conversing with the sommelier. I later learned she was choosing a bottle of Lugana DOC. The wine was supposed to marry well with her salad.

Whatever that meant.

Among the courses Madama ordered later were cinghiale in umido (wild boar stewed in Chianti and onions) and spinaci alla Fiorentina (Florentine spinach) accompanied by a bottle of Sassicaia 2000.

I guess that wine was supposed to get married to the boar. I don't know.

By the time she was enjoying her coffee and ciocolatisima (rich chocolate cake) several hours later, my stomach was making unseemly noises. It had been quite some time since I had enjoyed my ravioli with Rosina back at the albergo.

During her entire dinner, my Contessa had been flirting with several men, not all of whom were dining alone.

When she was waiting for her check, La Signorina shrugged her beckoning message to me.

I wondered if all she wanted was to give me a good hearty slap for all to see or for actual assistance on my part.

"Fido," she whispered. "Do not look now. But one of the diners here tonight interests me. He is quite pale, with a very aristocratic bearing. He is of athletic build and his dinner companion is a very tall Nordic creature wearing a high necked silver gown. They are sitting three tables away from me and are sipping some kind of *digestif* at the moment.

"I want you to discover who the gentleman's servant is. And when you do, inform him to let his master know that if he would like to contact me, the servant should let you know by telephoning you at the Albergo Gosso."

"Very well, Contessa. I shall see to it," I assured her with a bow.

Back I went to the flunky wall. This time without having received so much as a light slap on the cheek from my mistress.

Oh, dear.

I pointed out the table where the pale gentleman and his statuesque date were sitting to Gaylord.

"Do you happen to know if the gentleman's servant is among us here at the servants' wall?" I asked.

With a low-keyed, genteel chuckle Gaylord told me that not only was the servant present but that he himself *was* the servant.

"The gentleman, my master, is Lord Willowby Godshire. He is staying at the Palazzo Nicolini al Duomo. His family arrived in Britain with William the Conqueror in 1066. He is a member of one of the great noble families of England. A genuine blueblood."

The color of his blood was immaterial to me.

But I was interested in finding out about his Amazon date. Gaylord shuddered. He told me that he could never be so indiscreet as to reveal such personal information about the Milord or his guest.

I felt I had overstepped my bounds.

My apology was graciously accepted.

I told Gaylord that my mistress would not be offended if Lord Willowby were to attempt to contact her through me. And I gave him my telephone number at the Grosso.

By the time I had discharged my duty with Gaylord, I perceived that La Contessa had paid her bill and was ready to leave.

I hurried to her side as she departed. I believe every eye in the place followed her as we departed.

After the taxi stopped outside the door to her hotel, I opened the door for her and then beat my weary way back through the streets to my albergo and into the arms of Signora Rosina Pucci.

At midnight, Rosina and I were still frolicking in her nice soft double bed.

The telephone rang.

Damn!

Rosina answered right in the middle of an orgasm.

That guinea gal was really something!

"Yes," she told the person on the other end of the line. "I will go up to his room and have him come right down to talk to you."

Now all that was in Italian, of course.

"It's your Contessa," she told me.

It was, of course, also said in Italian. But the sentence was very close to its Spanish equivalent. And I would have gotten the point anyway.

I waited a suitable time, then picked up the phone.

"Yes, Madama," I said. "You called?"

"Yes, I called, you numbskull. How else could you account for the fact you are taking to me?

"Get into your pink livery and get over here to the Castello, *Subito!*"

Since she had taken on the role of Contessa, she had added a few words to her Italian vocabulary.

"Subito" was one of them.

The same word has a very similar meaning in Spanish. However, in San Diego, Spanish speakers would use the word "pronto" in a case like this.

I rushed back up to my room, donned my pink monkey suit, rushed out the door and got to La Contessa's suite in what I considered to be record time.

Even the late-night doorman recognized me and let me right in.

Madama was waiting for me in the lobby. She was attired in a full velvet dressing gown. And I knew what that meant.

Her leather dominatrix costume was sure to be lurking behind the velvet. I just knew without a doubt that the time had arrived for my Venus and me to visit the Castello's subterranean torture chamber.

Without a word, Madama turned heel and headed off towards a recessed portion of the lobby. I followed her down several hallways. She came to a stop before an ordinary enough looking door.

She had a key in hand and unlocked that door.

She entered a small room and, of course, I followed her. She locked the door behind us.

The light in the room was murky. But the trap door in the floor was visible enough.

My Venus inserted the key she had brought with her into the trap door's lock and stood aside.

There was no question that she expected me to step forth and open the flap.

I gave a good tug on the door and it opened right up.

Venus flipped a switch that illuminated the wooden planked stairway that led down into the baneful subterranean dungeon below.

And I followed her down into the chamber of horrors that awaited us at the bottom of the stairs.

The dungeon was filled with more instruments of torture than I could have imagined existed. The uses of most of them were mysteries to me. And yet, each was ominous and loathsome in appearance.

Venus removed her velvet dressing gown to reveal her leather costume.

While I stood dumb in the middle of the dungeon, she stepped over to an oak cabinet and removed a simple ancient horsehide whip. Its strands were gnarled, stiff and grisly. I knew that the smirches that stained the tail were remnants of dried human blood. An accumulation of gore that probably traced back to the fifteenth century.

A frisson of terror and submerged delight shot through my entire body at the sight of that whip and the speculations of ancient torture that it evoked.

La Contessa, with a sneer, invited me to sit in any of the three near-by inquisitional chairs. Each of the chairs was covered by spikes on the back, armrest, seat, leg-rest and foot-rest.

I chose the chair closest to me. I placed my shivering body into the infernal piece of furniture with great care.

The spikes jabbed me at every contact. But they were dull enough so that they did not penetrate my clothing or my skin. They were simply damned uncomfortable.

If I were not wearing my livery, I know those spikes would have been drawing blood.

This was the most uncomfortable seating arrangement I had ever experienced.

"An excellent choice of chair, Fido," my dominatrix gloated.

"The seat of that particular inquisitional chair happens to also serve as a grill. In the olden days, the inquisitor placed hot coals in the space below, so as to cook the ass of the victim while the spikes penetrated his body as it was pressed deeper and deeper into the spikes. The heat probably roasted the fellows balls rather painfully, too at the same time. Don't you think?

"Can you imagine the agony? A hideous nightmare for most. An approach to Heaven, perhaps, for martyr-minded masochists like you. No?"

It was a question that begged no response.

"In our more modern times, the chair has been improved by replacing the hot coals with electric burners. Don't you just *love* modern technology?"

Again. She did not expect a response as a sense of delicious horror overcame me.

"I wanted you to be exactly at this place, and in such a seat, when I explain to you what it will mean if you sign a contract to become my slave."

Contract? What was this about a contract?

"As far as anyone else knows," she explained. "You are merely my servant. Not my slave. But, your status will change to slave when and if you sign a contract to that effect. Once you sign, you will relinquish all rights of free choice.

"I will then be able to treat you far more abominably than I do now.

"I will be free to apply the bars that would press you deep and painfully into the spikes of that chair where you now sit as I plug in the electric heater to roast your ass and nuts. I could subject your putrid body to any of the painful instruments in this room. Without a qualm.

"Your expendable body will be mine to abuse, even unto a ghastly death when you are my slave.

"Can you even envision enduring my sadistic pleasure?"

As I squirmed in discomfort on the chastisement chair, my Venus plugged the heater below into a socket, producing a very low level of heat that invaded my butt and genitals. The sensation was that of sitting on the burner of a stove set at minimum temperature.

The feeling was not yet painful. Yet, it was terrifying when I considered the feeling when the heat would be at broiler level.

I was aware that this dungeon in which I was sitting had been in existence when Dante began writing his Inferno in 1308, not far from that very spot.

The poet was aware back then that if he did not escape from Florence soon, his enemies, the White Guelphs and the Cavalcanti family would capture him and inflict torture upon him. Perhaps in this very dungeon.

The prospect must have given him inspiration for the exquisitely written tortures he describes in his Inferno.

Even with the visions of terror that surrounded me, and my extreme discomfort, I looked directly into my mistress' eyes and responded:

"The worse you treat me, the more I adore you, Contessa. I become intoxicated and my soul becomes poignantly inflamed when you abuse, demean and beat me.

"I look forward with delightful anticipation to the moment when you deign to present me with a document to sign which will sweep me into a state of absolute servitude to you."

The expression on my Venus' face expressed such cruel delight that my slowly warming balls gave a clench of passion.

Madama unplugged the heating element that had grown in intensity to a point where it was likely that my satin trousers would soon become scorched.

"Get out of that gruesome chair, Fido," she commanded. "I would like to show you some of these exquisite torture devices.

"I have replicas of some of them already in my fazenda in the South American rain forest. And at the moment I have a group of Tuscan artisans copying some of the others for me.

"If you should become my slave in Surinam, you just might find that your life will end as the guest of one of the implements I want to introduce you to."

She led me to a box, or, rather, what appeared to be a sarcophagus. The face of a maiden was carved on it.

"Meet the Iron Maiden, Fido," she said. "An exquisite creation. Imagine what it will be like when you are entirely in my power and I decide to allow her to embrace you.

"Open the sarcophagus and let us explore the maiden's inner workings."

The box was hinged, so I opened it.

The interior was equipped with multiple spikes.

"I would like to point out some of the main features of the instrument to you, Fido, she said with an ominous grin.

"First, note that the spikes pierce quite specific parts of the body. Like here...*(She poked me on various sensitive spots of my body)*...and here... and...*(Cringe, cringe)*...here.

"You see, the spikes miss your vital organs so that you are not killed by them. You will remain painfully alive.

"A second feature of the maiden is that the space you are kept in is very confined. Oh, how that intensifies the suffering."

She swung the lid up and down for me.

"Another exquisite feature of the maiden is that it can be swung open and closed repeated, admitting the painful piercing again and again, by piercing to penetrate the same spots excruciatingly.

"As you can see, the maiden is not only a torture instrument. It can also be an execution device as the victim's blood seeps out of his body."

What a way to go.

In her guided tour of the torture chamber, she introduced me to the rack, the wheel, the thumbscrews (that work, of course, as toe-screws), the fingernail extractors, and enough more fiendish inventions of the human mind to give testimony to the kind of species we really are.

"Finally," she said, as she drew our guided tour to a close. "I would like to introduce you to a device that should intrigue you as an American."

She led me to a bench. "Here in Italy this is called the tocca. Your American CIA agents call it a waterboard. It is used for purposes of interrogation in your country. Here in this dungeon, it was used for that purpose as well. But it was additionally applied as a method of revenge or for execution.

"As it happens, the tocca is my favorite method of dealing with recalcitrant slaves back at my fazenda in Surinam. I use it on my slaves both as a method of chastisement and as an execution device."

What she was pointing out to me was probably the most innocent looking piece of equipment in the whole dungeon.

It was a rough, slanting wooden bench with five iron restraints. When the victim is placed on the bench, facing up, an iron restraining band holds down his forehead, encircles his neck, and clamps down on his arms and legs. The slant of the bench causes his head to incline downward. That is, the wretch's feet are raised higher than his head.

Beside this bench is a watering can. It is as innocent looking as the one that "Mary, Mary, quite contrary" is purported to have used to water her flowers. I noted that the can was full of water, and that there was a black colored towel folded up next to it.

La Signorina then delighted in giving me a rather detailed description of the history of the tocca and on the happy delights the torturer feels in implementing it.

The inquisitor places the towel on the victim's head to cover his eyes down to the bridge of his nose. The mouth and nostrils are left uncovered, of course.

The inquisitor pours water from the spout of the watering can over the face and into the mouth and nostrils of the captive. This causes the miscreant to believe he is dying. The forced water inhalation first causes him to gag and then to experience the actual visceral sensation of drowning.

The effect is not only one of terror. The pain is extreme. And the thrashing of the body against the restraints can result in broken bones.

The method, in various forms, goes back thousands of years. It was used in China in the Ming Dynasty and in Catholic Europe during the Inquisition.

Wanda, who saw herself as Dutch a well as Surinamese, was proud of the fact that the Dutch East India Company was using it to torture natives in the Molucca Islands back in 1623.

"Now," she concluded. "I want you to have the opportunity to experience waterboarding for yourself.

"I will attempt to stop the application of the water before you void your bowels and bladder. That is something that tends to happen to the victim after about twenty seconds of thrashing around. I am far too compassionate to cause you to wear befouled clothing when you go trudging back to your albergo later this evening.

"And it would inconvenience me greatly to have you break your arms or legs in the involuntary struggle that arises from the treatment.

"So, Fido," she asked. "Are you ready to endure the most voluptuous experience you will ever suffer in your life?"

I affirmed that I could hardly wait.

I cannot possibly even begin to describe the experience I underwent attached to that innocuous appearing bench.

It was the answer to a masochist's nightmare. I have met pain and terror before. As you know. But horror, mixed with the acute panic that wracked my mind, body and soul as I struggled to keep from death by drowning is absolutely indescribable.

La Contessa applied the water treatment on me for less than twenty seconds. Or, at least that is what she told me.

But now, years later, I still wake up late at night screaming from the experience.

When she released me from the bench I thanked my Venus for the most exhilarating moments in my entire life.

I glory in pain and terror. But the experience I had undergone exceeds the masochist's needs for pain, humiliation and terror.

And, on a minor note, when I got over my shakes and convulsions, I could not help but feel grateful that I had not shit my pants during the torture.

I came very, very close.

After she had educated me into some of the more arcane sadistic inventions of mankind, my Venus was willing to finish off the evening's entertainment with just inflicting a good old-fashioned flogging session.

She had me remove my clothes, of course.

Then she bound my wrists together with a length of rope and had me raise my hands up above my head.

She hung me by the wrists onto a hook that dangled on a chain from the ceiling. I was suspended, painfully, a few inches above the floor.

She still had the blood-stained horsehide whip in hand as she spun me around while I dangled from the chain. While I was whirling, she applied the thong of that scourge that bore the blood of countless martyrs to whatever vulnerable bodily part of mine that presented itself to her slashes.

Ahh! How pleasant to experience the kind of whippings I had learned to enjoy all my life.

I have to admit that I would never again willingly submit myself to waterboarding. Give me a good old scourging any time.

I put my clothing back on after La Contessa lowered me from my hook.

I followed her back up the stairs and back into the lounge.

"Be back here at the Castello promptly at eight tomorrow morning," she ordered.

"In the Castello kitchen you will find croissants and coffee. Bring them to my suite."

With a bow I said, "Very good, Madama," as I took my leave.

I staggered back to the albergo too beat and beaten to be able to do Rosina any good that night.

CHAPTER SEVEN

THE FATAL CONTRACT

At eight o'clock the next morning, I was in the kitchen of the Castello Cavalcanti al Duomo. The kitchen crew was quite accommodating, and they prepared Madama's breakfast most pleasantly and, even, artistically.

I was at the door of my mistress' suite before eight fifteen.

I knocked.

"Avanti!" she responded.

I opened her door and encountered her smiling and, oh joy! totally nude.

She did not demure in any way. My entrance was no more embarrassing to her than if I were a dog.

Well, after all, I was only Fido. A Fido bearing coffee and croissants.

I placed my tray on the coffee table in the living room and held a chair for La Contessa as she sat down to breakfast.

My eyes were held in fascinating focus on the gorgeous naked Surinamese Venus who slowly, graciously, and, yes, even suggestively, nibbled at her croissant and coyly sipped her coffee.

I was aware of the signs of entertainment in her eyes as she watched my prick trace its upward course in front of my satin trousers.

Her lips curled into an amused smile, knowing that the coquettish manner in which she partook of her breakfast was causing my pecker to throb in time to my accelerated heartbeat.

It pleased me that my unconscious carnal responses were so entertaining to her.

She did not mention my arousal by so much as a word. But every time her eyes glanced at my active crotch, she flashed her most beguiling smile.

"Today we are going museum hopping, Fido" she confided in me. "We will see some Venuses. I know how turned on you are by the love goddess. It shows all over you."

Was there a double entendre there? I thought so and consequently blushed. I believe to my own Venus' delight.

"We will also see some Davids," she continued. "Not painted, mind you. Statues. So they are not hung."

No question about it. That shot certainly had a double meaning. From the mischief in her eyes, I knew my blush at that remark elicited her mirth.

When she had finished her breakfast, I hustled Wanda's tray, loaded with her used eating implements, back to the Castello's kitchen.

The staff there, as before, very graciously received the tray back.

What lovely people those Florentines are.

When I got back to the Signorina's suite, she was in her bedroom dressing herself for our outing.

When she returned to her living room, she was very modishly attired. Naturally.

"We will begin at the Galleria del' Accademia," she informed me. "It is over on Via Ricasoli, a walk of ten minutes or so."

And right she was. In somewhat less than ten minutes we were at the entrance to the Accademia.

We went through the lobby and took a left turn. And there we were in the nave.

There are a lot of Michelangelo's unfinished statues along the sides of the aisle, but Madama showed no interest at all in those. It was the enormous statue that presided over the far end at the hall that held her spellbound. Yep. Michelangelo's David.

I've got to grant you he's big all right. At least fifteen feet tall.

And he's buff, as well. Looks like he worked out regularly at the gym.

But his prick! My God! What a teeny weenie!

My first reaction was that the dude couldn't do much good for a woman.

And yet, as we approached him, La Contessa's eyes were fixed only on the statue's crotch.

I've heard, time and again, people say that size doesn't matter.

Perhaps they're right. But somehow, the big marble youth's dong was clearly speaking somehow to my Venus.

I looked at La Contessa's face as she stood less than six feet away from the giant statue. She was absolutely transfixed. Tears were streaming down her face.

And her eyes were still fixedly staring at that cock.

Then, I realized something about what she was gazing at. The cock was small, in comparison with the body. But that marble dildo, if removed from the rest of the statue, could give my Venus a real ride for her money.

When she'd dried her tears away, we exited the Accademia.

Our next stop, the Uffizi Gallery, was also within easy walking distance. It was down on the Arno River.

There's an outdoor terrace café before you get to the entrance of the Uffizi. Madama decided to stop there for a cappuccino and a pastry. She did not permit me to enter with her. So I stood outside.

I knew she was aware that I would really enjoy a snack at the time. So, before entering the terrace she told me, "Man was born to suffer. And you, Fido, in particular, need to wallow in suffering. None of the great martyrs were given feasts. Not even crumbs. So wipe that mournful look off your face. If you need to get stuffed, get yourself back to your provincial San Diego. You are perfectly free to leave here at any time, you know."

I had not realized that my hunger showed.

So I put a happy expression on my face and said, "Buon Appetito, Contessa" to her as she entered the café to enjoy a coffee and a snack.

At least, standing outside waiting for her, I had a splendid view of both the Duomo (Cathedral) and the Palazzo Vecchio. Food for the soul.

When she finished her snack, my Venus came back out onto the street, delicately wiping her lips with a napkin.

We walked through a courtyard to the entrance to the gallery.

Once inside, we hoofed it four long flights up a staircase to the top floor. The ascent nearly caused me to have a nosebleed.

Madama was unfazed by the climb.

What a woman! What a goddess!

We proceeded down the hall and ducked into the first door to the left.

The room we entered had a collection of early Italian paintings. You know, that dull Medieval stuff. Flat paintings by Giotto and those other religious painters back in the 1200s and 1300s. I could do without them. But Madama stood before each picture with apparent enjoyment while I squirmed.

Oh well... *De gustibus*... and all that.

There were three rooms filled with all that early religious crap we had to get through.

Bored me silly. But then, I was only Fido, so it was my job just to tag along and keep my big trap shut.

Finally, we got to the rooms with paintings done in the 1400s.

This was more like it. That is to say, less boring to me but still intriguing to La Contessa.

It took us nearly an hour to get through gawking at *those* pictures. But we finally got to the rooms that had stuff painted from about 1450 to 1500. Now *this* was more like it. This was where the Botticellis were hanging.

That Botticelli dude was a painter after my own heart. His model was his mistress and his goddess. God, what a gorgeous hunk of womanhood she was.

When we got to his painting of the *Birth of Venus*, I actually wept.

That painting was doing for me what the statue of David back at the Accademia had done for Madama. It mesmerized me.

No, my reactions went beyond mesmerization. I stood there, transfixed, and fell in love. This was a Venus to rival my own. Her right hand was raised into a position where it should be wielding a whip. Venus' left hand was masturbating her snatch. And that lovely goddess was staring directly at my groin.

That long moment standing before the greatest artistic masterpiece of all time made the whole trip to Florence a true religious pilgrimage for me.

The hardon I sprouted was nothing less than sacramental. I came close to creaming my pants.

I was suffering a deeply religious experience!

The Leonardo da Vinci stuff in the next room was a letdown. But, then, to be fair, anything would have felt mundane after Botticelli's *Birth of Venus*.

The next room we visited had a couple of surprises for me. Two statues of Venus were standing there waiting for me.

The first one was the *Venus de' Medici*. It's a marble sculpture of a nude Venus in the same pose Botticelli portrayed in the *Birth*. It pretty much shook me to the core until I turned around and... Oh my God! What a mood-pooper.

I was looking at a statue called *The Venus with a Penis*.

It was enough to make you want to puke and send you scurrying for the exit.

There wasn't really anything else in that museum that I was really interested in until we got back down to the terrace.

La Contessa let me go in and sit with her there. I think she actually had taken some kind of pity on me after my experience of exaltation at the two Venuses I had worshipped and my subsequent abject depression when that God damned *Venus with the Penis* knocked me for a loop.

What *my* Venus ordered for each of us in that café was called *The Little Cappuccino Monk."*

It's a cappuccino decorated with a swirl of chocolate that creates a face on the foam.

As we sipped our cappuccini, Wanda and I relaxed from our roles and actually smiled lovingly at each other.

That intimate moment was never to occur between us again.

La Contessa was hungry soon after we left the Uffizi and she had a lunch of pasta and salad at the Mescita Fiaschetteria over by the Accademia. I got a panino from a street vendor to satisfy my own ravenous hunger.

Our day as culture vultures continued after Madama's lunch break.

"Come along, Fido," she urged me. "I want to take in the Bargello next."

It took us only a few minutes to get to that sculpture museum. It is over on the Via del Proconsolo.

The Bargello is a three story building.

We had to climb the stairs to get to the room Madama wanted to see. That's the Donatello room.

The Signorina was interested in the statues up there. But they all left me cold. Particularly Donatello's bronze *David.*

Sure, the statue was a trend setter way back when. It was the first free-standing male nude sculpted in Europe in over a thousand years.

Great! But this particular *David* was a sissified teen-ager with a pre-pubescent weenie. And clearly as queer as a three dollar bill.

I'd always had a question in my mind about the relationship between David and Jonathan in the Bible. Donatello was clearly on the side of the two being homosexual.

Now don't get me wrong. Homosexuality doesn't bother me one way or another. Although I am straight, myself, I suspect that there might be some people who would find my own sexuality a bit kinky.

"Live and let live" I always say.

But, anyway. I thought it was nice to find out that an artist back in 1430 clearly had come to the same conclusion I had about David's gay feelings about his good buddy, Jonathan.

However, I did not feel a need to share my personal observations with my mistress. It was my job to please her. Not to annoy her.

After we left the Bargello, we spent the rest of the afternoon visiting the Palazzo Vecchio, the Duomo, the Baptistery, the Ponte Vecchio, the... Well. You get the idea.

We *did* the town. Tourist style.

After we'd finished with as much as our tired feet and legs could handle, La Contessa sent me back to my albergo.

She claimed she wanted to be alone. Fine!

I loved that woman fiercely. But after a full day of tramping around ogling at cultural icons, I was ready to call it a day and get myself a bit of nookie with my Rosina.

And, as I knew she would, Rosina met me with open arms and thighs.

That evening, as Rosina and I were engaged in a round of sport, the telephone rang.

Wouldn't you know? The ring burst into the bedroom right in the middle of one of Rosina's wild orgasms.

Not too strange, come to think of it. That woman was the most multi-orgasmic creature I'd ever fucked.

The caller was an English speaker. And he wanted to talk to me.

I was on the verge of coming myself at the time, but took the call.

Rosina relieved my mounting tension by jacking me off as I spoke to whoever the untimely caller might be.

Turned out it was Gaylord.

"Hello, Fido?" he was saying. "Hope I'm not calling at an inopportune time..."

I didn't respond. I was just on the brink of erupting in response to Rosina's nifty maneuvering with her fine Italian hand.

Gaylord pressed right on, ignoring my lack of response.

"Lord Willowby instructed me to inform you that he wishes to invite..."

"Ahh!"

I could not restrain the exclamation that accompanied my ejaculation.

"Hello, hello, Fido, old chap! Are you quite all right?"

I assured Gaylord that I was very much all right. But explained my outburst by claiming that I had just attempted to stifle a sneeze.

He was reassured by my lame response and continued.

"As I was saying. My master would be pleased if you were to transmit to your mistress his invitation for her to join him for tea at the Palazzo Nicolini al Duomo tomorrow morning at ten o'clock."

I assured Gaylord that I would pass the information on to Madama. But I told him not to expect a return call.

Madama either would be there or she would not.

Gaylord was satisfied with that and signed off.

I immediately telephoned La Contessa and told her about the invitation. She made no comment one way or the other.

But I later discovered that she had accepted His Lordship's invitation. Because:

I received no summons from Madama the next morning to fetch her her breakfast.

And, as the day progressed, there still was no call from her.

Evening fell on Florence, and I had not received any call from La Contessa.

Not that I was bored by being restricted to the charms of the Alborgo Grosso all day long. Signora Pucci, my landlady, kept me happily entertained every moment of the day.

At dinnertime, Rosina and I were sitting at her kitchen table downing capellini pomodoro followed by chicken Parmigiana. Oh, how that wondrous woman could cook!

We were lustily gulping down her vino da tavola to accompany the fine feast.

And wouldn't you know it?

The God damned telephone rang.

It was, of course, my Venus. She told me to get into my pink livery and get my ass over to the Castello "*subito!*"

So I swallowed a last sip of the wine, kissed Rosina and gave her a slap on the ass. I rushed up to my room to get into the pink monkey suit.

When I arrived panting at the Castello, the manager on duty recognized me.

After all. How many guests had lackeys running around in pink eighteenth century costumes?

"Madama la Contessa is expecting you in the dungeon," he told me in flawless English.

"Do you know the way there?"

I assured the good fellow that I could find my way to the room which was billed as a "historic Inquisition museum."

When I wended my way down the murky stairs to the grim dungeon, Wanda was standing there in her dominatrix garb and with that grisly horsehide whip in her hand.

And standing behind her, naked as jaybirds, were two guys.

One was Lord Willowby.

He was as handsome as I remembered him. And as buff and ripped as if Michelangelo's *David* had come to life.

And, to my delight, the guy had as tiny a dick (in proportion to his size) as the God damned statue.

A bigger surprise to me than his lordship was the other dude. He was Milord's dinner date from the other night. Same face. But very clearly, he was not the female I had taken him for when he was sitting in the restaurant in drag. The person standing before me was, indeed, a statuesque Nordic. A strapping Viking. But instead of appearing like a fröken, he was a big husky male Swede by the name of Bjorn.

And, to my regret, Bjorn was hung like a horse. The size of his bundle more than made up for his buddy's paucity in that department.

Now it was clear to me.

Willowby and Bjorn were queers. And Bjorn was also a transvestite as well as a homosexual .

"Remove your garments, Fido," Madama ordered. "I wish to introduce you to my two good friends."

So off came my satin duds and I was soon as nude as the English lord and his trusty Viking sweetie.

The two guys gave me the onceover up and down my body. They clearly liked what they saw. Each one licked his lips lasciviously.

Uh-oh!

After they'd made their visual sweep of my nudity, their eyes rested hungrily on my crotch and glistened with some kind of unholy anticipation.

La Contessa introduced me to them. I probably would have made the effort to shake hands with the boys, but gave up the idea when I found I could not make eye contact with them. They were too riveted on my dong to be interested in such niceties as shaking hands or mouthing something banal like "Nice to meetcha."

I could not help but notice, however, that their peckers were stirring upwards to salute me.

My own dick was, if anything, retreating ungraciously up into my pelvis. Maybe that's why all those statues Wanda and I had seen in the Florence museums had such small penises. Their dicks may have shriveled up like mine was doing because the hunks aren't sexually interested in any of the tourists out there gawking at them.

"Now, Fido," my mistress told me. "I brought you here to test your servility. I know you can bear a great deal of physical punishment. That is a necessity for anyone I could even consider for servitude. Verbal abuse and humiliation seem to agree with you well. Those, too, are attributes of a worthy slave.

"But now I want to see you submit yourself to something that I know will be most disagreeable to you. You must do this to demonstrate your absolute devotion to me. Something that goes against the grain for you."

Uh-oh! I could tell what was coming next. The two hunks were clearly growing hornier and hornier.

My Venus was going to make me fuck those two fairies. And I would have to get fucked by them as well.

This was stretching my masochism to the extreme. If I had to pay that price to show my submission, did I *really* want to abase myself to that level?

I was wavering for the first time. I seriously considered walking proudly out of that dungeon and leaving all my dreams of masochism behind.

I knew that Wanda was scrutinizing my indecision. This was likely the ultimate test for me that she had in her book. Would I or would I not jump through this final hoop?

I looked at the genitalia of my two nude inquisitors. Their equipment was pulsating in anticipation of an orgy with me as the virginal treat. The sacrificial victim to their lust.

I knew that my own pecker had shriveled as though I were standing up to my hips in freezing water. I felt like one of those God damned mini-pricked statues.

I wondered whether I could even perform if I decided to go ahead with what my Venus was clearly asking of me.

I understood the unspoken command.

I hesitated. I trembled. I was unsteady on my feet.

And then, I made my decision.

Without her having to tell me what she wanted of me, I did the unthinkable.

I marched right up to the English lord and grabbed his face in my hands and forced him to look into my eyes.

Then, I brought his face to mine and kissed him on the mouth.

When he stuck his tongue in my mouth, I wretched and gagged.

Wanda and the two boys laughed, and then clapped.

Next I stepped up to the big Swede. I knew I could not bring myself to put my lips to his.

He stood quite still wondering what I was going to do.

I was wondering myself.

I stood directly in front of him reached my right hand out and encircled his massive rock-hard prick. I gave it a few masturbating pumps and released it.

There!

Wanda was not going to be satisfied with that.

"Bend over and kiss it!" she ordered.

I gritted my teeth, swallowed hard, and complied.

I gagged. My stomach lurched. And up it came.

I urped the contents from my queasy belly out onto the floor.

My three inquisitors roared with laughter.

There were mops, rags and buckets in the dungeon. And I knew what I had to do.

As I cleaned up my own mess, Wanda and the boys were laughing and joking quite merrily.

And, of course, I was the object of their mirth.

Once I had cleaned up the floor, my Venus was ready to proceed with her torture.

She directed that I be a participant in what Lord Willowby called the Game of Lucky Louie.

The game was a three man sex romp, with me playing the part of "Lucky Louie," the chap in the middle.

The setup was to be that Bjorn would be fucking me in the ass while I was cornholing His Lordship, who, for his part, would be jacking off.

But, lamentably, no matter how hard I tried, and no matter how accomplished the boys were in fondling and sucking at me, I was absolutely unable to raise a hardon.

"Well, Fido," La Contessa concluded. "If you can't, you can't. You proved that you would have consented to that final indignity if your puritanical body had allowed it."

Puritanical me? What a concept!

"I know it is a great disappointment to Lord Willowby and Fröken Bjorn that you turned out to be impotent, Fido.

"But we will compensate for your inadequacy by simply whipping you to a froth."

Oh, what blessed words. No more gayness!

What I really needed right then was a good whipping.

And that is what I got.

I was painfully bound to a crucifixion cross.

Wanda still had her grisly horsehide whip in hand. Lord Willowby had a flipcat and Bjorn had a bullwhip.

And those three laid it on me good.

Delicious!

My three inquisitors took rapid turns flogging me.

I was hanging facing away from them since my back was the target. And for a fair while, I delighted in knowing who was the current tormentor as each lash slashed in turn into my skin. La Contessa had previously made my epidermis well acquainted with the antique horsehide whip. And I had long before distinguished the difference between the sting of a flipcat and a bullwhip.

It was a good ten to twelve minutes before the pain from my floggings managed to tease my prick out of its reticent withdrawal. Once thus stimulated, my recessed dick blossomed into an excited erection.

My Venus had chided me a quarter hour before for being impotent. She had even said I was "inadequate."

Under the teasing of the cruel scourges of her and the boys, I certainly proved myself both potent and adequate.

My ejaculations coated the upright beam of my cross until it glistened before the eyes of the inquisitors.

Before I fainted, I had become exalted into a state of transcendence.

I came to, lying on my side on the floor before the cross that had sustained me during my flagellation.

Wanda was standing over me admiring the bloody streaks with which she and her two darling companions had decorated my back.

The boys had taken their leave during my comatose state.

So I was happy to find myself alone with my adored goddess.

She gave me a little kick to the ribs with the tip of her sharp-pointed stiletto-heeled boot.

"Bravo," she said.

It was the first and last time she ever congratulated me.

"You came through the final testing of your adequacy...well... adequately.

"Get your scrawny ass over to one of those inquisitional chairs."

I managed to wrench my aching body up off the floor and chose one of the chairs that did not have that ass-heating application.

There's nothing like variety, is there?

I was sitting very gingerly on that God damned chair with its nasty spikes pressing against my bloody, bruised back and butt.

Wanda approached me with a sheaf of papers in hand.

"Well, now, Fido," she smiled.

My discomfort was clearly quite evident to her.

"The moment has come," she told me.

"I wonder if you're ready and willing at this time to sign your own death warrant.

"Do you think you realize now what it would mean to be absolutely under my power?"

I assured her that I had realized it for some time and still desired to submit to her unconditionally.

She handed me the papers she was carrying.

"Read these documents," she ordered. "If you agree to the conditions stated, you may sign the three copies of the contract."

I read the contract, word for delightful word.

"I, Leo Messick, bind myself to be the absolute slave of Wanda van Domme until such time as she herself sets me free. I am to bear the name Fido. I am unconditionally to comply with every one of her wishes and to obey every one of her commands. I am to be submissive to my mistress without exception.

"Madame van Domme is entitled not only to punish her slave as she deems fit, even for the slightest infraction, but is given the right to torture him at her slightest whim simply for her own amusement. Should she so desire, she may kill him mercilessly.

"The undersigned agrees that he is unconditionally her property.

"Should Madame van Domme ever chose to set her slave free, I promise never, under any circumstances to consider vengeance or retaliation."

That was the document and I happily signed each precious copy.

"That is scarcely the end of the legal work, Fido," she told me.

"You must now read the next document very carefully. It is your suicide note. After reading it and considering what it may portend, you are to copy it in your own handwriting. Not once, but twice. And sign each of those copies as well.

"Naturally, you must not date the note. I will take care of that after you die."

Sitting on that spiked chair and doing all that reading and writing was quite an ordeal. Yet, I accomplished the task in what I considered a noble manner.

The suicide note read as follows:

"I, Leo Messick, having grown weary and disillusioned with life, hereby put an end to my worthless life. The local government may dispose of my remains in any way it sees fit."

I signed the copies. But, as per Wanda's directions, I did not date them.

It was comforting to know that the date would be added when, or if, my goddess ever decided that I was too much of a bother for her to keep alive.

When Wanda had all the copies of the documents in hand, she dismissed me.

"Go back to your albergo, Fido," she ordered.

"I am through with you for now. But I want you back here in this dungeon at midnight tomorrow.

"We will have one last Florentine session then."

So, I gathered we would be off for Surinam within days. A place where I would *really* be a slave.

A situation I had longed for all my life.

I had regained enough strength to follow Wanda out of the dungeon, close up the place, return the key to her and head out into the streets of Florence.

When I got back to the Albergo Grosso, Rosina was sitting up waiting for me.

Without asking me any questions about how I happened to have bloody slashes all over my back and butt, she anointed me with salves and applied bandages, put me to bed and held me in her arms until I fell into a blessèd sleep.

The next morning was the beginning of my last day in Florence.

I told Rosina that La Contessa had informed me that my stay was coming to an end. And Rosina took very good care of all my needs throughout that day.

At midnight, I reported to Madama in the Castello's dungeon.

She had me disrobe and sit in one of the inquisitional chairs.

"So, Fido," she said. "Here we are in our new status, owner and slave.

"You will discover that you have not really known me before. You have thought I have some positive feelings for you, you fool.

"I laugh at you. I despise you. You are now nothing but my plaything. You are now my slave, at my mercy, and mine to kill at my merest whim.

"I am sending you off on your way to my fazenda tomorrow morning at eight o'clock. You will leave for Rome on the train."

She handed me a train ticket.

"I will have a car waiting for you there when you get off the train. The driver will take you out to Leonardo da Vinci-Fiumicino Airport. He will give you your plane ticket to Paramaribo. When you arrive in Paramaribo, my slavemaster, Wim van de Kamp, will meet you and take you to my fazenda deep in the southern rain forest.

"I will remain here in Florence for a while. But when I am though with my business here, I will find you in the slave quarters in Surinam.

"Good bye."

I had been dismissed.

I got dressed and left La Contessa standing there in that dismal dungeon.

I had a train ticket in my hand and the freedom to do whatever I chose to do until eight o'clock the next morning when I would board a plane for Rome.

I spent the day in sweet dalliance with Rosina Pucci.

CHAPTER EIGHT

SURINAM ENSLAVEMENT

When I got off the plane in Paramaribo, customs was a snap. As baggage, I had only a small suitcase and there was very little in it.

At the gate there were quite a few people waiting to greet returning friends and relatives.

But I had no difficulty picking out the person in the crowd who was expecting me.

Wanda had told me that her slavemaster, Wim van de Kamp, would meet me at the airport.

And the pair of eyes that bore in on me as I exited the customs gate had to be said Wim.

He was a large, blondish white man attired completely in white and was wearing a pith helmet. He had an extremely ugly scarred face.

But the thing that distinguished him most clearly from everyone else in the crowd was what he was carrying in his left hand. It was a coiled black bullwhip.

Wim van de Kamp was holding that whip the first moment I saw him.

And, for as long as I knew him, I never, ever, saw him without it.

I walked right up to him, carrying my suitcase.

"Wim?" I asked.

"Follow me," he replied.

He turned on his heel and headed for the exit doors.

I followed him out into the parking lot and to a black Land Rover.

He got in on the driver's side.

I tossed my bag in the rear and got into the vehicle on the passenger side.

Wim seemed to be the strong silent type, so I did not attempt to initiate any conversation as he drove us through the streets of Paramaribo to a heliport at the edge of town.

I kept stealing glances at his face when I could do so unobtrusively.

It was disfigured by multiple knife wounds, most of which appeared to have healed a long time before. There were, however, a couple of slashes that seemed to be still in the process of healing.

That Wim, I figured, was one tough cookie.

At the heliport, he parked the car and we got out. I retrieved my suitcase from the back seat.

A black attendant approached us. Wim spoke to him curtly in Taki-Taki and we followed the chap to a helicopter.

Wim ascended into the pilot's seat. I got in on the other side, tossed my bag into the space behind my seat and wondered what was going to happen next.

Wim took over the controls, and before I knew it the copter rose straight up into the air.

Once we started heading South, Wim suddenly became communicative.

His tone was neither friendly nor hostile. It was harsh and matter-of-fact. He neither smiled nor frowned.

And yet, there was something harsh and cruel about the man. He frightened me.

He informed me that he was Meesteres Wanda's slavemaster.

A fact I already knew.

He told me he spoke Dutch, Taki-Taki and English. And was able to communicate somewhat in some of the Indian dialects of the southern tribes of the country.

I asked him what Taki-Taki was. He told me the official language of Surinam is Dutch. But that twenty-two languages are spoken in the country.

Taki-Taki evolved from the languages of several African tribes. It was brought to the country by the slaves back in colonial days. Dutch and English terms got woven into the speech. He informed me that Taki-Taki was the most prevalent tongue used in the country.

It was the only language he used with his slaves, except when Meesteres Wanda acquired a European like me from time to time.

Now that he had broken from his previous verbal brevity, he decided to inform me about his relationship to me.

He let me know quite forthrightly that his job was to keep slaves like me docile and obedient.

Then, he grew quite wordy for him.

"We are heading for Fazenda Macabra. That is Meesteres Wanda's plantation in the rainforest down near the Brazilian border," he told me.

"When we arrive there, I will give you a solid flogging in front of the other slaves. That will be your initiation into the group of vermin of which you are now a part."

Well. It was nice to know what was going to await me in my new home.

As we progressed southward, the scene below morphed into a deeper and deeper green.

My slavemaster now took on the role of a rough-spoken tour guide.

He told me that the territory we were headed for was a vast territory that stretched from the south shore of the Tapanahoni River to the north shore of the Amazon. That it was the densest tropical rain forest in the world and was still, even in the twenty-first century, largely unexplored.

It is a land of trackless forest and unmapped rivers.

The rains fall daily. And at times they descend ceaselessly for weeks.

Seeing the rain forest grow denser and denser as we progressed gave me a deep, sensual thrill. Down there, Nature still ruled unabated. The thin garb of civilization that the Earth wore elsewhere had never infiltrated that wild wet land below.

To be a true slave in that dense, luxuriant territory would be, for me, a dream come true. Just the kind of land for a deep-dyed masochist like myself.

At length we landed in a small clearing in the jungle.

When I got out of the helicopter with my bag, Wim took it from me.

"You won't have much use for anything in there for a while," he informed me. "I will keep this until the Meesteres determines that you need it."

I nearly said "thank you." But the expression did not feel particularly apt.

A narrow path had been cleared from the landing spot into the dense foliage that engulfed us.

"I will introduce you to these forest surroundings before you disrobe to receive your first beating," he told me.

"Come along to the fazenda. I want to show you the slave quarters. Your new home."

He led me along that path for approximately a quarter of an hour.

At length, we arrived at the enormous fazenda.

The main house was an extensive one story building. In addition to the dwelling, there were stables, corrals, out-buildings and gardens.

To the west of the main house there were three of the meanest looking shacks I had ever seen anywhere.

"Home for you," Wim exclaimed as he nodded towards the wretched appearing quarters. I knew immediately that those were the slave quarters.

In front of the shacks there stood an upright pole.

"Whipping post," Wim explained.

There was a fire pit close to the pole with a metal rod standing in it.

"Branding iron," I was told.

Oh-oh! Nothing had ever been said to me before about a branding iron!

Standing in front of the center shack was a group of totally nude individuals.

"Slaves like you," Wim explained.

There were nine of them standing docilely in a line staring at me – four male and five female. They were all around my age.

I could not distinguish any predominant racial features that would define the group. I guessed they were of mixed races. I would have to classify each one of them as a Negroid-Indian-Creole mix of races and ethnicities.

There was one unifying characteristic they all had. All of them were *beautiful* people.

My Venus obviously demanded handsomeness in her slaves.

Now that I was joining them, I was the only Caucasian in the group. A minority of one.

Wim addressed them. I believe he was introducing me. But since he spoke to them in Taki-Taki, I could only pick out a few words. The ones that sounded like English words.

I asked him if anyone of my fellow slaves spoke or could understand English.

"No," he told me. "No English. There are a few words of English and of Dutch in Taki-Taki. But if you want to talk to any of your fellow dogs, you will either have to teach them English or learn Taki-Taki yourself. Good luck."

I knew there was no way any of those naked creatures was going to learn English. And I did not see how in the world I could learn any Taki-Taki other than picking out the bits of English that had sneaked into the tongue.

I envisioned a lonely servitude.

Wim led me to the middle shanty of the three buildings. The slaves stepped aside to give us ingress.

The interior of the building was even more depressing than the exterior.

There were eight wide wooden beds inside. There were no mattresses or covers lying atop the rough planks that constituted the sleeping frame.

And that was it. Other than the primitive beds, there was no furniture. No tables, chairs, wall pegs, lights, candles or lamps graced that room.

This was home to my nine fellow slaves. I would be the tenth resident.

Eight beds. Ten occupants. I wondered how that would work out.

After I had taken in the amenities of my new home, Wim led me back outside.

"Before you get comfortably established here, Fido," he told me. "I will take you on a walk through the surrounding forest. I want you to see for yourself that there is no possible escape for any of the meesteres' slaves. Come along with me!"

And so, I went for a tour of the neighborhood with my slavemaster.

I followed along behind Wim out of the compound and onto a narrow path that led into the looming forest. I knew Wim considered me of no more worth than a little dog. So I, Fido, trotted along behind him.

Rain began to fall. It was a warm rain. And I was soon soaked to the skin with muggy dampness.

Wim appeared to pay no attention to the water falling on us from the skies and dripping down from the branches overhead.

With the bogginess, the forest seemed denser, the trees larger and the undergrowth more abundant.

As abruptly as the rain had begun, it ceased.

As soon as the downpour stopped, there was a buzz of what must have been millions of insects. Floods of birds flew from tree to tree. There were rigalajos, toupals, toucans and parrots. All of them were decked out in eye-dazzling colors.

Monkeys up in the trees began to squeal at us.

The undergrowth of mosses, ferns, creepers, fronds and low shrubs constantly threatened to invade the narrow paths we followed in an attempt to stifle us.

Wim pointed out an anaconda dangling from a branch.

Watch out for snakes overhead," he advised me.

"The anacondas are mean. But they are nothing compared to the camoodi who coil about a branch and are the color of the tree itself. One of those near invisible creatures could crush your bones like brittle twigs in their constricting coils."

Now there *was a scary thought.*

"But don't keep looking upward for safety," he went on "Poisonous snakes, like cassaries, slither along the ground you are walking upon."

He told me about the aripita, a species of wild boar that inhabits the jungle. And he advised me to watch out for jaguars. To say nothing of hunting leopards that tear animal flesh to tatters in a minute.

A huge agaguato, a howling monkey, jumped down onto our path and scared the shit out of me.

Wim laughed.

"Don't worry, Fido," he told me. "The agaguato is just trying to be friendly."

We wandered around following trails that led into other trails.

The rain started up again as we approached an Indian village.

"These are our nearest native neighbors," he informed me.

The village I was looking at consisted of a bunch of hovels made of twigs and leaves. The hovels surrounded two large mud structures. The entire village was surrounded by water, marsh and, of course, the ever present forest.

There were a few natives sitting under a kind of leafy canopy near one of the mud structures.

I could tell the Indians decidedly were not friendly.

"Any slave who attempted to escape from the fazenda would eventually reach one of these villages," Wim told me. "He would end up being eaten by those cannibals."

As we wandered on through the labyrinth of narrow soggy trails, Wim continued to warn me of the myriad horrors that awaited fugitive slaves.

Little did he know that his horror tales did not affect me one bit.

After all, I had consciously and enthusiastically chosen servitude to my Venus.

I knew that in due time, she would return to Fazenda Macabra where I could again worship her by submitting myself to her merest whim.

Why in the world would I ever consider escaping?

My whole purpose in life was to grovel at my mistress' feet.

And, until her return I was willing to yield to her vicar who ruled in her absence – Slaafmeester Wim.

By the time we got back to the fazenda, the rain had let up.

I felt like a drowned dog as I trudged behind Wim back to the slave compound.

My fellow slaves were assembled near the whipping post.

And I noticed that coals were glowing in the branding pit.

It looked like party time to me.

"Remove all your clothing, Fido," Wim ordered.

"It is time for you to be initiated into your new status. Your companions over there are anxious to see how you measure up."

I removed my soppy clothes from shirt to shoes. I stood before my Slaafmeester and my fellow slaves in full unadorned splendor.

I looked each one of my fellow thralls in the eye.

I believed I detected a welcoming gleam in the eyes of each of them.

Wim ordered me to hug the whipping post, which I did eagerly.

With a piece of rope, he bound my wrists together.

My legs were not shackled in any way.

"I will apply a dozen lashes to your back, Dog," he advised me.

"You need to know the fury of my whip."

As he flogged me, my fellow slaves counted out the strokes.

I was not able to remember the names of the numbers as they were called out in Taki-Taki.

I was too engaged in being delighted by the fierce sting of each of Wim's strokes with his whip.

When Wim had applied the twelve strokes to my bare back, he untied my wrists. As I turned about to face him and my companions, I exhibited a glorious erection.

Wim seemed unaffected by my priapic condition.

But I could tell that the slaves all approved of what they were witnessing before their marveling eyes.

I had a pretty good idea what was in store for me next. The branding iron was sitting in the fire pit and I was stripped naked. The kind of pain I was in for would be novel. And, frankly, it was something I would have willingly shunned.

The thought of a glowing hot iron being pressed into my skin caused my hardon to shrivel away fast.

I wondered where I would be branded.

I had not yet detected any brands on my fellow slaves. Could it be that I had been uniquely chosen for the honor?

If so, why?

I did not have long to ponder this question.

"Lie down on the ground, face first," Wim ordered.

Well. Here goes!

I complied with the order.

As soon as I was sprawled out in the dirt, two of the slaves held down my legs, two others held my arms. And two others sat down on the middle of my back.

Their weight on my back pressed painfully against my welts. It was nearly enough to take my mind off of what I was about to suffer.

I was firmly pinned down securely to the ground by the efforts of my fellow slaves.

I knew that was a good thing. While being branded, moving around convulsively could prove disastrous to my skin.

When that God damned branding iron pressed down on my right ass cheek, I let out a scream that set the monkeys in the nearby forest to howling up a storm and launched a thousand parrots into a flurry of fluttering and squawking their heads off.

Those sounds did not drown out the sizzling hiss of my own skin as it was being cooked.

And the stench of my burning flesh was downright sickening.

My comrades who were holding me down sprang away from me as soon as the iron was removed. They were anxious to get up and admire my newly acquired decoration.

When I glanced up, I noticed that all the slaves sported a brand on the same location on their butts as mine had been scorched. A letter "W" was embossed on each slave's ass.

I guess I should have been delighted to have become one of the gang now. But I certainly would have been happy to have foregone that pleasure. The searing pain remaining from the branding smarted for a very long time after the deed was done.

Wim left the scene after he had set the branding iron back among the glowing coals. So I was free to get acquainted with my newly acquired comrades.

They managed to demonstrate to me in a variety of non-verbal ways that they were happy to have me as one of their company.

I did my best to show as much bonhomie as my painful concerns allowed.

By then, it was an hour or so before sundown. The slaves were through with their tasks for the day as far as I could tell.

The men indicated that I should follow them into the shanty that stood to the left of what I knew to be our dormitory.

I accompanied them into the building while the four women headed over towards the groothuis, which was what everyone called the enormous living quarters of my mistress, my lovely owner.

The building we male slaves entered tuned out to be our dining room or messhall. There was a long, rough-hewn table dominating the room with rough-grained benches on each side of it.

My companions sat down at the table. I would not have been able to set my throbbing, burning ass down onto one of those rough planks for the life of me. For, though I thrive on pain, I could not convince myself to set my burning ass down on that rude bench with my fellow slaves.

So I kneeled on the bench and attempted to make a friendly face.

The men engaged me in conversation by trying to teach me words. They pointed to objects like the table, the bench, the wall, the door and so on and encouraged me to repeat the Taki-Taki word for the objects after them.

Naturally, I was unable to remember hardly any of the words on that first trial. But that attempt at a lesson was the beginning of my adventure of learning the lingua franca of Surinam.

Before too long, the women arrived back at the messhall bearing cauldrons of the food we were having for dinner that evening.

They set the food on the table. The women sat down, and we all began to eat.

I thought the food was the most ghastly mess I had ever tasted. I had not had a bite to eat since I had deplaned in Paramaribo. So, with the length of time that had passed and the extensive walking through the thick rain forest, I was certainly hungry enough.

But as hungry as I was, eating what seemed to me to be slop proved to be a chore.

I learned soon enough that we slaves received two meals a day. One meal was served not too long after dawn and the other about an hour before sunset.

The recipe for all our meals was fairly simple. As a new diner at the messhall, I did not know what the gunk even consisted of. I later discovered that the ingredients of our meals consisted of the following:

The base of the concoctions served to us slaves consisted of boiled cassava, plantain or tayer. Cooked into that base there were hunks or shreds of meat or fish. The meat was purchased from one of the hunting tribes of the area. It could be the meat of a monkey, opossum, snake, jaguar or parrot... The list of possibilities could go on to include every species that inhabits the jungle.

I tried not to imagine what kind of meat was purchased by our owners from the cannibal tribes.

Masochism only goes so far.

After dinner, we all got up and went outside.

My companions sat on the ground facing west. I knelt down beside them keeping my smarting ass well off the dirt.

As the sun was setting, my mates began singing.

The rhythms and beats were unlike any music I had ever heard before. The songs were neither chants nor melodies, but a format like something between those two forms.

But the effect was absolutely beautiful.

Eventually, during my stay at the fazenda, I learned to sing all the slave songs that were a part of our daily life.

Every evening, after dinner, we faced the setting sun and sang that gorgeous music.

I spill a tear even now as I recall and recount those beautiful musical moments that accompanied the tropical sunsets.

We did not go to the dormitory until the rim of the sun's disk set over the tree tops of the verdant forest.

There was enough afterglow from the sunset so that I could make out my companions features inside the shanty. They paired off, male-female, as they settled as couples onto the rough-planked beds.

I crawled onto one of the empty beds and lay down on my stomach to avoid causing pain to my aching back and butt.

I faced away from the wall.

The pairing off left one woman standing next to the beds by herself.

The light in the room was disappearing fast. But I could make her out well enough to know which of the five women she was.

And she was absolutely lovely.

Just before darkness overcame the room, I saw her nod at me.

I nodded back and felt her slip onto the bed beside me in the absolute pitch darkness that fell upon the room when the last gleam of sunlight disappeared.

I rolled over onto my left side to face her. I was reluctant to make any other move as an overture until I could get a feel for what my role was in this new venue I found myself in. I thought that any actual physical contact should be initiated by her.

I felt her fingers reach over my shoulder and lightly graze the nape of my neck.

The spot right at that hollow is so sensitive and so erogenous that a charge of electric current shot down my spine igniting a titillating spasm at my tailbone.

I reached out my right hand, clasped the back of her skull and drew her head close to mine.

Holding her head with my left hand, I caressed her cheek with the fingers of my right hand.

In response, she drew her hand from the back of my neck and placed the tips of her fingers lightly on my own cheek.

All the pain that I had felt where the lash and the branding iron had marred my skin was forgotten in that moment of romantic sensitivity.

I traced a circle around her lips with my forefinger. When she reciprocated I gently probed along the sensitive location where her lips met. She sucked my finger into her mouth and ran her tongue around it.

She placed her pinkie finger in my mouth. I extended my tongue out to greet it. As I lathed that delightful little digit with my tongue she coyly slipped it into my mouth. My tongue followed it back into my oral cavity. As I sucked it, my tongue played love games.

I ran my finger in and out of her mouth as she sucked even harder and played ever more erotic games with her skillful tongue.

When my finger was massively lubricated, I pulled it slowly and lovingly out of her mouth and began to draw light arabesques around the aureole of one of her nipples. She gasped with delight when I twisted, turned, pulled and pinched the nipple until it was extended to its utmost.

In response, my partner withdrew her finger from my mouth and held her palm over it so I could lick it and tickle it with my tongue.

When her palm was fully moist, she withdrew it from my face.

What was she going to do next?

As I lowered my mouth to suck that fully protruded nipple of hers, my new sweetheart's saliva-lubricated hand slipped down the length of my torso, skipped over my throbbing hardon and gently coddled my balls.

My entire body was consumed with bliss. I could no longer think. I could only feel.

My hand reached down to cover her snatch. It was warm, moist and inviting.

My pecker was urging me to enter her tunnel of Venus. But a stronger urge bade me run my middle finger up and down her slit.

Those cunt-lips yielded lovingly to my romantic peregrinations up and down their dewy surfaces.

My lover's gentle grip released itself from my nuts. And I jumped, somewhat startled, as her thumb and forefinger encircled the base of my boner and massaged me there.

Good Lord! I did not want to come yet. I wanted to come only inside the warm cunt I was handling.

I was pretty sure I could hold back until I had a chance to spend some time paying homage to her clit.

I gently lifted the clit-hood and ran loving fingers up, down and around that precious jewel that nestled there.

At that point, she encircled my dickhead with a grasp that suggested, unequivocally, "mount me."

My woman twisted away from the braced position on her side and dropped flat onto her back.

As she took that position, I arose, positioned myself above her, got my knees into position between her spread legs and lowered myself, slowly. I was still in desperate need, until my peckerhead caressed my sweetheart's warm moist labia.

I intruded into the divine passageway inch by inch at first. Then with a barbaric thrust I made my full invasion into the depths of her womb.

I wondered at first whether the sounds of ecstatic delight we uttered as we came and came amused the couples occupying the other beds of our love bungalow.

But then, on the other hand, I was aware somewhere within the depths of my consciousness that similar sounds emanated from all the other beds. Our room companions were also all young and lusty.

"Fido," I whispered to my love when I extricated myself from our embrace.

"Roona," she replied.

And thus, still in the throes of our rapture, we introduced ourselves to each other.

Roona and I did not get much sleep that night. There were simply too many exciting ways to play get-acquainted games.

However, when dawn broke, we found that we were awaking in each other's arms.

I still loved my Venus, of course. But I also fully embraced this magical love affair that fate had thrust upon me.

With sunrise, the new routine of my servile life commenced.

It was made up of coarse food, oppressive heat, constant humidity, blood-sucking insects and lashings galore. The hard labor of hacking, sawing, digging, planting and harvesting was unending.

On the plus side, Roona was teaching me Taki-Taki as an accompaniment to our lovemaking. That was pillow talk at its best.

I was learning the sunset songs that ring joyously in my head to this very day.

And I was cheered by daily thoughts that my Wanda would be returning home soon.

The anticipation was so sweet.

A month passed with me lovingly counting each day in anticipation of Venus' return to her Fazenda.

Then, one morning, when Slaafmeester Wim roused me out of bed with a sharp poke to the ribs, he told me Meesteres Wanda was back and desired to see me.

Ah! The moment I had waited for had arrived.

Now the whole purpose of my life could be resumed.

To serve my goddess directly with abject submission to her will.

CHAPTER NINE

BLOSSOMS IN THE DUST

I followed my Slaafmeester to the Groothuis with my heart beating double-time in happy anticipation of seeing my Venus again.

The interior of the mansion was more ornate than I would have guessed. There were oriental rugs on all the floors. The furniture was an eclectic collection. It was made up mainly of French antiques, generally favoring Louis XV. But quite a bit of Empire and even later styles were mixed in as well.

All the rooms were quite large, of course. I would have liked to take some time to stop along the way and admire the mansion. But Slaafmeester Wim kept moving through the place at a brisk pace, and I knew better than to lag behind.

When he got to the door of Wanda's bedroom, he knocked three times.

"Ja," my owner responded.

When Wim announced himself, she told him to enter.

Communication between my Venus and my slavemaster was usually conducted in their common language, Dutch, of course. But when Wim told her I was with him, they both changed over to English.

"I have brought your new slave here to serve you, Meesteres," Wim explained.

"Oh, it's you, is it Fido?" she addressed me languidly.

Her voice came from behind the curtains of a four-poster Louis XIV bed.

Even without having seen her yet, I felt my body quiver in delight.

Wim withdrew from the room and closed the door behind him.

"Where is my breakfast, Slave?" she asked me quite abruptly.

Although the question was a bit unreasonable, since I had not been given a clue that I was supposed to arrive with food, I apologized.

I did not even know how to address her there in Surinam. I gave it a try, though.

"I am sorry, Madame," I replied humbly. "I will bring you some immediately."

"Do not address me as Madame, you idiot," the voice from behind the curtains scolded. "Do you think you are still merely my servant? Do you think we are in your country? Or in Europe? You are such a dunce. I don't know why I put up with your stupidity. I am your mistress...your owner now. Meesteres Wanda, or even simply Meesteres alone may suffice as titles when you are privileged to address me at all. Do you think you can remember that, you moron?"

"Yes, Meesteres," I said. I added a deep reverential bow to my response even though I was pretty sure she could not see me from behind those bed-curtains.

"I will return immediately with your meal."

I exited the door and attempted to guess where the kitchen might be in this enormous edifice. I knew we had not passed through it on the way from the front entrance to the bedroom.

I took an educated guess and was lucky. I made good choices in direction and ended up in a beautifully appointed kitchen.

When I got there, there were three young ladies bustling around in the kitchen. They all smiled at me as I entered.

I did not know whether they were servants or slaves. I later learned that all the house servants at the fazenda were slaves. But I also found out that they lived in the groothuis, not in the slave quarters.

The one of the three girls who seemed to be in charge asked me a question.

"Ontbijt?"

I did not know whether the word was Taki-Taki, Dutch, or both. But I correctly guessed that it meant breakfast. So, I answered in what I hoped would be intelligible to her.

"Meesteres Ontbijt," is what I came up with.

The lovely young thing nodded and answered, "Jawel . Meesteres Ontbijt," and handed me a tray consisting of pastries and slices of mango and papaya. She then went to an urn and poured freshly brewed coffee into a pitcher and placed it on the tray.

I was not ready yet to attempt to thank her in whatever language the two of us were speaking. So I bowed, smiled, and headed back to Meesteres Wanda's boudoir with her breakfast.

I hoped I would eventually be able to speak to that lovely chocolate-color skinned kitchen maid.

I was in love with Wanda. And, I was in love with Roona. And was also ready to fall in love with the kitchen girl in due time.

She was a real knockout.

I returned to my meesteres' boudoir bearing her tray.

I set the edibles and coffee out on her breakfast table in an orderly fashion. There were some attractive pastries, some mango and papaya slices and her coffee to arrange.

Since Wim had led me to the groothuis before the slavegirls had brought the morning slop to the slaves' messhall, my stomach was making rude noises complaining of hunger.

But that was of little concern to me. And, of far less concern to Meesteres Wanda.

Wanda pushed open the bed-curtains and addressed me.

"Well, well, Fido," she said. "I must say that nudity becomes you. I have always found something bizarre about dogs whose owners dress them. Do not worry. I will not put clothes on you except when propriety absolutely demands it."

That was fine with me. Modesty was hardly my forte.

"Crawl over here on your hands and knees, now," she commanded. "I require some pre-breakfast hors d'oeuvres."

That was a new one to me. What in the world are pre-breakfast hors d'oeuvres?

I crawled towards the bed, attempting to appear as canine as possible.

I looked up at my meesteres and stopped dead in my tracks.

She was nude! There was not a stitch on that voluptuous, blonde, alabaster-skinned, gorgeous body. Her long golden hair flowed enticingly down over her round pale shoulders framing those perfect rose-tipped breasts.

Doggie got a hardon!

"Now that you are mine, body and soul," Wanda told me. "Your signs of submission will graduate from kissing my foot to a higher level of subjugation.

"Prior to my breakfasting and consequently garbing myself, you will pleasure me with cunnilingus and annilingus.

"Do you understand the terms?"

"Yes, Meesteres," I acknowledged. "I understand."

"I see that your condition is ithyphallic," she sneered. "I suppose that is inevitable. However, I hope you understand that you are not to commit any onanism in my presence. Unless, of course, I specifically order you to abuse yourself."

"I understand, Meesteres," I acknowledged.

"Fine, then, Fido," she ordered. "Hop up here onto the bed, kneel humbly between my spread –out knees, and employ your tongue and lips in a manner to bring me to a glorious climax."

O, joy! Oh, Bliss! Those would be acts of devotion beyond my wildest hopes or dreams! I was born to be a slave.

The delta of soft, blonde, downy pubic hair that graced my Venus' mount was so fragrant and inviting that, despite myself, I had to nuzzle a cheek down into it. Wanda gasped, but did not scold.

I rolled my head around so my lips could graze over that soft, lovely scented welcoming pubis.

With my tongue and lips, I traced that triangular tuft down to the northern tip of her vulva.

Ahh! Now I inhaled the most beautiful scent in God's creation. The musky odor of cunt.

I nearly swooned.

The tip of my tongue tickled the upper reaches of the divine slit.

Wanda had not informed me whether I could touch her with my hands and fingers. I decided to risk her displeasure and spread those outer lips so my tongue could reach the rich juices that had accumulated just within the portals of Heaven.

My meesteres was not displeased by my action. I could tell from the soft sighs of contentment that escaped from her mouth.

I ventured to lift the hood that masked her clitoris to pay homage with tongue and lips to that ruby of Paphian delight.

My antic tongue played myriad tunes and traced wild arabesques up, down, in, out, flickering and lingering over every sensitive, erogenous nerve-tingling area of that holiest area sacred to Venus.

Despite all her dignity, Wanda squirmed, wiggled, lurched, shimmied, moaned, yelped and shuddered.

I brought her to three consecutive orgasms through the medium of my lips tongue and fingers.

She had to order me off her cunt or I would gladly have continued my ministrations all day long.

"That is sufficient, Fido," she told me abruptly.

"What I desire now is to determine your skill at annilingus."

Was I ever ready!

I scooted towards the back of the bed so my love could assume the position which would give me ingress to my next target.

She curled down, forehead to the surface of the bed, knees tucked up against her lovely belly and ass aimed at the ceiling.

It was enough to give a fellow a blue woodie.

I crept up upon that beckoning Mecca with infinite stealth. I wanted Wanda to tremble with anticipation. I knew she desired the thrill of not being sure just when my slavering tongue would strike.

When I was poised within striking distance, I rested a hand on each of her nates.

She quivered.

I placed a thumb on each side of her posterior cleavage and pulled the delightful moons apart.

And there it was. Exposed to my enamored eyes.

A little, puckered, rosy bud. It pinched together and, by God!, I swear it winked at me.

As I settled my lips down towards that darling, tiny asshole, the delicate sharp, musty scent completely intoxicated me.

My senses had already been excited by the cunt-smell while I had laved her snatch. Now, to mix bum-smell into the other olfactory delights was enough to nearly cause me to swoon.

To begin with, I just barely flicked that anus with the tip of my tongue.

Delicious. Delirious. That sharp, tangy flavor is unlike any other in the universe.

Following the flick was a tongue-flutter.

I ran my tongue over the rosebud as rapidly as my lingual muscles allowed.

Wanda could not hold still. A trembling coursed through her body. She squirmed with such jolts that it took all my strength to hold her ass steady so I could intrude my tongue into the tastiest region of all, just inside the sphincters.

As with the cunnilingus, I would willingly have spent the entire day glorying in that annilingus.

But my Venus apparently was satisfied with a quarter hour's worth of those hors d'oeuvres before breakfasting.

She ordered me off the bed and then arose herself.

She donned a peignoir, walked over to her dresser and picked up an envelope and proceeded to her breakfast table.

She did not comment on the homage I had paid to her evacuative organs. But I was sure she felt I had been skillful enough and submissive enough to provide a pleasant wake-up experience for her.

As I stood quietly, and as unobtrusively as possible next to a window, my meesteres daintily sipped her coffee and nibbled at her food.

When she had dabbed the last drop of coffee from her divine lips, she curled a finger at me.

I responded by approaching her with a smile and a bow.

She handed an envelope to me.

"Here, Fido," she commanded. "Take this letter to Meester Maarten at Fazenda Boekwoud.

"And, as you leave, take this tray of dirty dishes with you."

"Yes, Meesteres," I replied with a bow. "Immediately."

With the letter and tray in hand, I bowed my way out of the room and shut the door behind me.

I went to the kitchen to return the tray with a severely painful case of lover's nuts bothering me.

The attractive young lady I had taken such a shine to in the kitchen took the tray from my hands and gave me a mischievous wink.

When she laid the tray down, she pointed to herself.

"Koozna," she said.

"Fido," I replied.

And thus, we introduced ourselves. I hoped it was the beginning of a beautiful friendship.

She indicated that I should sit at the kitchen table. Which I gladly did.

When I was well seated, she brought me a tray loaded with the same kinds of pastries and fruit as my Venus had eaten. But in much greater quantity.

She carried over a pot of coffee and poured me a cup.

I dove in, since it was by far the best food I had eaten since I had arrived in Surinam.

After she had poured me my second cup of coffee, Koozna pulled up a chair next to mine, took a slice of papaya from the tray with her left hand and rested her right hand on my thigh.

Oops! I sprang an immediate hard on.

Koozna giggled.

She signaled that I should continue eating. She began nibbling on her papaya as her delicate chocolate colored hand explored my cock and balls.

Oops, again!

I came in her hand.

After all the erotic play I had exercised with my meesteres, I had built up a need that had been about to burst my nuts.

Koozna thought my premature explosion hilarious. And, with a handy napkin, she cleaned up my mess.

I tried to grab a handful of tit, but she demurred.

I made a second attempt, but she sent me from the kitchen with such determination that I could not refuse her insistence that I leave.

I said "Dank" as I left.

She replied with a nod as she pushed me out the door, making smacking sounds with her lips as she did so.

To this day, I cannot recall a more delightful breakfast in all my life.

As I walked into the groothuis' living room, Wim entered from the front door.

I showed him the envelope Wanda had given me.

"The meesteres handed me this envelope and told me to deliver it to Meester Maarten at Fazenda Boekwoud," I told him.

"Then deliver it to Meester Maarten, Stupid," Wim replied acerbically.

"But Meester," I explained. "I do not have any idea where Fazenda Boekwoud is. Or how to get there."

"You get there by running, Fido," he told me. "The meesteres takes a dim view of any courier of hers who walks rather than runs.

"The fazenda is only some five kilometers distant from here, so you should be able to get there without over-exerting yourself.

"I will set you on the path that runs there directly through the rain forest. Even a stupid oaf like you cannot possibly get lost on the way.

"But *do* try to get there alive. You don't appear to me to be too alert yet about the dangerous creatures that haunt our forests."

He led me to a path that led into the dense jungle.

As I began to run down the path, the sharp sting of Wim's vicious whip hit my butt.

I resolved to keep my senses acute with my eyes wildly looking all about me for any signs of snakes, jaguars, wild boars or other dreadful monsters.

But the remembrance of the glorious experiences of licking Wanda's twat and asshole, and of Koozna's jacking me off kept me somewhat distracted along the way.

I was surprised at how soon I arrived at that neighboring fazenda. I ran all the way and was not winded at all.

The setup of Fazenda Boekwoud was not too unlike Macabra. It had an extensive groothuis, decrepit slave quarters, barns, stables, orchards and fields. The slaves were toiling in the fields and there was a servant at the door of the groothuis observing my approach with suspicion.

The servant must have announced my coming for before I got to the massive front door, a young man stepped out into the open.

There was no question the gentleman was the meester. He was elegantly attired and extremely handsome.

He had brown hair, brown lively eyes and was of athletic build.

I was jealous.

He saw the envelope in my hand.

I extended it to him. He looked me up and down contemptuously and arrogantly.

"You must be Wanda's new slave," he said to me in accented English. "She tells me you are an American chap.

"You make quite a bizarre sight popping around nude out to the forest bearing messages from your owner."

I did not answer him. Nor did he seem to expect one from me.

He opened the envelope and read the enclosed letter as I stood there like a lump of stupidity.

I began to entertain doubts about what I had let myself in for in coming to this country as a ridiculous appearing slave.

"Hmmm," Maarten commented when he had perused the letter.

"Your meesteres has invited me to join her for lunch today. Inform her I would be delighted and will be at her fazenda at eleven-thirty."

He turned around and re-entered the building, leaving me standing there feeling extremely foolish and stupid.

I hit the trail back to Wanda's and gave her Maarten's answer.

"Wonderful," she said. "I will have you serve us when he gets here.

"But you cannot possibly do so appropriately running around with your lavaliere hanging out like that."

She laughed her wicked laugh.

"No, no, no," she continued. "I do have a livery here for you."

She went to an armoire and found a white linen outfit and a pair of sandals for me.

"Here," she said, handing them to me. "Take these to your slave quarters. Then report to Wim. He will want you to work in the fields this morning.

"Return here at eleven o'clock in uniform to serve Maarten and me. And, for Heaven's sake, wash the dirt and sweat off your body before you get back here."

There was no underwear and no socks in the bundle Wanda had given me. I reasoned that an abject slave like me would hardly need such refined amenities.

We slaves were allowed to bathe in the stream that ran through the plantation, so I would be able to comply with my Venus' order to return cleaned and appropriately attired.

I returned to the fields to join my fellow slaves. And I arrived back at the groothuis clean and in my linen livery at the appointed time.

The kitchen staff had prepared a delightful lunch which I brought, tray by tray, to an open-air dining area located at the south wing of the mansion.

I hustled back and forth from the kitchen with my trays of food and drink.

I felt like a non-entity as the handsome couple conversed and joked in Dutch and laughed a great deal.

I could not understand a word they spoke, but it was clear enough they were ridiculing me as I bustled about.

At one point, as I was serving them wine, I inadvertently spilled some Chateauneuf-du-Pape. It fell not only on the linen tablecloth but a drop also besmirched Wanda's gown.

She slapped me smartly on each cheek, causing me to reel.

Maarten doubled over with laughter at my discomfort.

Wanda looked at him, pointed at me, and joined into his hearty laughter.

I humbly simply continued serving the food and wine as best I could.

I began to wonder if slavery really suited me as well as I had previously anticipated.

The next morning, Wanda informed me that she was throwing a dinner party that evening at six. And that I would be the serving boy.

When the time came, I was back in livery, rushing back and forth from the kitchen to the formal dining room.

There were six male guests at the party, including Maarten.

There were five female guests. And, of course, Wanda, as hostess rounded out the party.

I was very careful not to spill so much as a drop of wine anywhere. I still felt the humiliation and consequent laughter that had occurred at the patio luncheon.

It was a bright cheerful crowd. There was laugher aplenty. And I felt certain that a great deal of the gaiety was directed at my apparent clumsiness.

I was feeling less and less enchanted with my life as Venus' slave and devotee.

I longed for a more conventional form of masochism.

The party broke up late in the evening.

Maarten and another young man remained after the others left.

One of the ladies stayed behind as well.

I was told to go to Wanda's bedroom when I had finished cleaning the dishes from the dining room back to the kitchen.

And to arrive back there nude.

When I reported for duty, nude, with great apprehension, I was shocked at how dissolute the group of young people appeared.

"Oh, Fido," Wanda exclaimed when I entered the room.

She was clearly quite drunk and, I must say, unattractively so.

"We are all having such a glorious time," she said in slurred tones.

"And it is about to become even more delightful because we all want to get ourselves inflamed for the orgy to come."

"And you are going to help. Because we are going to all get a chance to whip you.

"Won't that be fun?"

Now, I suppose there is no one on earth who enjoys a good whipping as much as I do.

But being a whipping boy buffoon at a party of profligate drunken debauchees did not, in any way, define my idea of a pleasurable pursuit.

Each member of the drunken party took turns flicking that blasted whip at me. I was not bound or shackled, but was just urged to walk and stumble about the room as the revelers took turns at attempting to land a stroke on me amid their riotous laughter.

I did not enjoy a single stroke. Not even from my goddess who seemed to me to be the most shameless participant in the group.

When the lewd party was over and the guests had all left, Wanda wanted to talk to me.

"Fido," she said. "You know what?"

"What, Meesteres?" I replied.

"You bore me. That's what. You're no fun. My friends are fun. Maarten is lots of fun.

"He's the kind of man I have looked for all my life. A man who can dominate *me*. Not some fucking milksop like you.

"*You* don't even deserve to be here in this house, you sap.

"Get out of my sight and back to your filthy slave quarters."

I trudged back to my bed in my quarters extremely depressed.

This was not the life I had in mind when I fell in love with my divine goddess.

I reported to Wim the next morning. He put me to work splitting rails with a heavy ax.

So there I was standing out in a bare field, nude, miserable, and wielding an ax, as a deluge was pouring down on me from an angry sky.

What the Hell was I doing there?!

Day after dreary day dragged on.

One day we slaves were gathered near the whipping post to witness the initiation of a newly acquired slave.

He was a muscular black male. Standing still, he could be taken for an ebony statue representing heroic, massive strength.

We slaves silently watched him get beaten and branded.

And we led our new brother into the messhall to enjoy our morning slop.

The new arrival spoke Taki-Taki, so he was immediately involved in discussion with the others of our kind.

We all toiled away the rest of the day in the fields. We returned for our evening mess and then went outside as usual to chant as the sun set over the tops of the trees of the forest.

When we went into our quarters, I lay down in the bed Roona and I had occupied since I had arrived.

Roona went to one of the empty beds with the newly acquired slave.

Those two and the other couples fucked for hours.

I whiled away the dark hours crying and jacking off.

Thereafter, day followed day in morbid loneliness.

I did not see Wanda. I did not see Koozna. And Roona became a stranger to me.

The days dragged on interminably. The weeks melted into months.

Then, one morning, Wim jabbed me in the ribs with the handle of his ever-present whip as I awoke.

"The meesteres wants to see you, Fido," he informed me gruffly.

"Get your ass moving. She does not like to be kept waiting."

What now?

I ran to the groothuis and proceeded directly to my Venus' bed chamber.

This time, she was fully dressed when I arrived.

I kissed her foot.

"Oh, get up, you Ass," Wanda grumbled.

"I want to talk to you. Sit down!"

This was a new approach.

"How do you like your life as a slave?" she asked me.

"It is not quite what I had anticipated, Meesteres," I told her honestly.

"I do not have any further use for you," she went on.

"I need a lover, not a dog. And I find that Maarten is so perfectly virile that he more than suffices as my lover.

"Wim finds you nearly useless as a plantation slave. And you are demoralizing to my other slaves.

"So, if you wish to return to your home in San Diego, I will willingly release you from your contract, destroy your suicide note and have Wim put you on a plane which will whisk you out of my life."

Well, *that* sounded like an offer I could not refuse.

So, I returned to San Diego and got my job back at the library.

And, at the moment, as I write this, I happen to be on vacation.

Yes. I am back at the Pancho Villa Hotel here in Zihuatanejo.

Yesterday, I was beaten by one of the ugly whores here in my dingy room.

But, when I awoke this morning, I had a strange premonition that my life was about to enjoy a change.

With a sense of happy anticipation, I donned my fancy attire, actually primping myself up like some kind of fancy Don Quixote out to encounter the Dulcinea of his dreams.

So, in a few moments, I will head out the door for Ixtapa with spritely step.

For, I know with a certainty that Fate will be leading me off to that specific place for a reason.

My friends. I tell you truly:

There is no armor against Fate.

ABOUT THE AUTHOR

TIM DESMONDES

Tim Desmondes and his wife reside in Southern California.

Tim is the author of eleven books other than the present volume published by the Nazca Plains Publishing Company:

- *Sex and Loathing in Hollywood*
- *Sexual Diversity and Perversity in California*
- *Dracula Sucks Hollywood Dudes*
- *Venus Does Adonis While Apollo Shags a Tree*
- *Arthur Does Camelot*
- *Whores, Love and Pistols in the Wild West*
- *Robin's Too Tight Tights*
- *Sex and Love in Paris and Frisco*
- *Agnes Sorel: The Breast and Crotch that Changed History*
- *Beowulf, Wulfgar and Their Friggin' Horny Gods*
- *Colleen O'Merry - Dominatrix to the Stars*

If you enjoyed *Wanda the Whip Lady* you might want to enter Tim's world where you will meet other characters who have shared their stories with Tim, who, in turn will share their stories with you.

Desmondes

Agnes Sorel
The Breast And Crotch That Changed History

Agnes Sorel

a novel by
Tim Desmondes

Desmondes

Arthur Does Camelot

Arthur
Does Camelot

a novel by
Tim Desmondes

Beowulf, Wulfgar and their
Friggin Horny
Gods

Beowulf, Wulfgar and their Friggin Horny Gods

a novel by
Tim Desmondes

Desmondes

Dracula Sucks
Hollywood Dudes

Dracula Sucks Hollywood Dudes

Tim Desmondes

Desmondes

Inside Robin's Too Tight Tights

inside
ROBIN'S
too tight tights

a novel by
Tim Desmondes

Desmondes · SEX AND LOATHING IN HOLLYWOOD

Sex and
Loathing in
HOLLYWOOD

Tim Desmondes

Sex and Love
in Paris and Frisco

Tim Desmondes

Desmondes · SEXUAL DIVERSITY AND PERVERSITY IN CALIFORNIA

Sexual Diversity
and Perversity in
California

Tim Desmondes

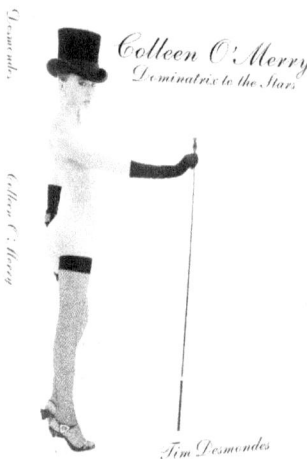